The arct
descended in an icy rage

Snow as hard as sand, driven by gale-force winds, pummeled the men with ceaseless brutality. It was time to bail out of the frozen hell.

Katz radioed Jack Grimaldi, who was waiting fifty miles north in a helicopter.

The reply signal was weak. "Can't get to you," Grimaldi's voice crackled amid the static. "We're socked in here...it's the blizzard of the century...sorry, guys...hang on...."

The radio signal died.

Katz clicked off his walkie-talkie and turned to the others, his eyes haunted.

"The blizzard of the century," he muttered, despair gripping his face. Phoenix Force was alone with the storm. Had they survived this far for *nothing*?

"Gar Wilson is excellent. Raw action attacks the reader from every page!" —*Don Pendleton*

Mack Bolan's
PHOENIX FORCE

Mack Bolan's
ABLE TEAM

MACK BOLAN
The Executioner

PHOENIX FORCE

AN EXECUTIONER SERIES

White Hell

Gar Wilson

A GOLD EAGLE BOOK FROM

W🌐RLDWIDE

TORONTO · NEW YORK · LONDON · PARIS
AMSTERDAM · STOCKHOLM · HAMBURG
ATHENS · MILAN · TOKYO · SYDNEY

First edition July 1983

ISBN 0-373-61306-7

Special thanks and acknowledgment to Thomas P. Ramirez
for his contributions to this work.

Printed in Canada

1

Mass murder—premeditated and ruthless—was only a heartbeat away.

And Seattle would never be the same.

It was 3:45 P.M. on a clear December day in the Pacific coast metropolis, and rush-hour traffic on Interstate 5 was particularly dense. With Christmas only four days away, there was an electric excitement in the air. The sun, a flat, orange cutout, was sinking toward the smog-smudged skyline.

Salesmen, plumbers and electricians, secretaries and businessmen, mothers returning from last-minute shopping, from school Christmas programs—all became unsuspecting grist for the impending bloodbath.

Matt Redfern and his terrorist cutthroats realized that Phoenix Force was hot on their tail. Abruptly their 1978 Toronado was goosed to a yawing, squealing, sixty-mile-per-hour flight. The sedate afternoon joyride suddenly became a run for life.

"Keep on them, David," Katz barked, "don't give them a blasted inch."

"Right-o, Yakov," McCarter acknowledged, his knuckles white on the steering wheel, eyes darting as he sought to wedge into the steady lines of traffic. "If I don't kill me a few blokes in the bargain, it'll be a bloody miracle."

He leaned on the horn, swerved, bucked and bluffed his way into slot after slot. Right. Left. Cutting off a silver-haired matron in a Lincoln Continental. "Move it, lady!" he bellowed. "Get that goddamned beer truck off the road."

The squeal of tires, the blast of the horn, the grind of steel on steel as he shoehorned his way into a gap between a Toyota and a Ford—all were music to McCarter's ears.

Knowledge that a bloodthirsty contingent of the IRA was in the United States, spoiling for a showdown, had been in Stony Man Farm's intelligence circuits for the past forty-eight hours. A hit at the Seattle docks, near the oil-refinery tap lines, had been accepted by Hal Brognola and company as the general scenario. A messy little blowup to draw America's attention, to warn that the IRA meant deadly business—that was how the men of Phoenix Force had read it.

Smug bastards, Katz thought to himself. To be suckered in so easily.

The Phoenix team had contented itself with a round-the-clock stakeout, maintaining a discreet distance between its chase car and the Toronado used by Redfern and his five hardmen whenever they left their seedy Pioneer Square hideout. It was essential to Stony Man's strategy—and that of the big guy, Colonel John Phoenix—that the IRA terrorists be caught in the act.

But now, suddenly, sickeningly, everything was blowing up in their faces. They realized too late that the IRA showdown would not come at some sparsely populated cargo-ship loading dock, but in a public arena, where the body count would be horrendous.

Armageddon on the freeway.

It had been Rafael Encizo, his psychic antennas eternally alert, who had first become edgy. As the lemon yellow Toronado had plugged through heavy Yesler Way traffic and eased onto the I-5, heading south at leisurely pace, something had begun to bubble within him. And when the terrorists blithely bypassed the Harbor Island turnoff, where the strike was supposed to take place, things suddenly went to high boil.

The Toronado exited on Empire Way, taking a pokey detour that meandered through Jefferson Park, as if the terror goons were pausing to take a last grim breath, to rev up nerve for the mission. It was in the park that an IRA lookout had been alerted. Catching glimpse of the blue 1981 Chevrolet Impala tailing them, he yelled a warning to his mates.

Instantly the pace had quickened.

Blasting back onto the freeway, heading north, Redfern opened up the Toronado, the car fishtailing through lanes with hair-curling bravado.

And when Phoenix Force had seen the assault rifles poke their ugly snouts above the window rails, the IRA hoods craning their necks, the driver deliberately prowling a lumbering gasoline truck in the left lane. . . .

"They're gonna do it right here," Rafael gasped. "The bastards are gonna blow away half the goddamned city, us included."

"They wouldn't dare," David McCarter shouted, his mouth twisted into a vengeful snarl, his powerful arms spinning the Impala's wheel with a proficiency gained from hundreds of outings on the race circuit. Driving recklessly, he jammed the sedan into a space that seemed hardly big enough to accommodate a motorcycle. "There are kids, women in those cars. What kind of animals are these blokes, anyway?"

But the terrorists did dare, bulling themselves into position beside the huge tanker, jack-rabbiting into opening after opening in the heavy traffic. The IRA driver had gained a lead on the truck. Once their ugly job was done they could escape to deliver a crowing victory message to a disbelieving world.

The IRA lives. Bloody as hell.

And unless Phoenix Force could break through the glut of doomsday drivers and stop them. . . .

Gary Manning furiously peeled down the back window, poking his craggy face out into the IRA car's slipstream. His tawny hair flattened against his head, the CAR-15 panning the landscape, he sought a firing angle amid the blurred intermesh of vehicles. A young blond mother on the sidewalk saw his weapon and instantly reacted. Her mouth gaped in disbelief, and her right arm shot out to protect the tyke strapped into the kiddy-carrier beside her.

Manning interpreted her dismay, his heart constricting at thought of the gory trick destiny would shortly play on the attractive woman and her baby. *Sorry, lady,* he groaned inwardly, still straining for a shot, *I didn't make this damned, stinking world.*

An angle presented itself and Manning, praying that no innocent blood would be shed by his hand, brought the sighting leaf down, zeroed in on the Toronado.

"Shoot, Gary," Katzenelenbogen shouted into the back of their vehicle. "Don't let them get a round off." Then he swiveled back to lean halfway out the front window on his side, deftly manipulating his prosthetic hand, aiming across the windshield. His Colt Commander .45 barked twice and took down an IRA hardman in the front seat. In the rapidly fading light he inventoried the havoc he created as the slug tore away the man's skull, blood and pulp spraying the windshield.

Simultaneously, Manning opened up, stitching a fifteen-round line across the Toronado's rear and right side, carrying up into the windows, glass shattering like diamond confetti in the fading sunlight. The double dose of slugs caused the IRA driver to swerve slightly. Momentarily out of control, the Toronado bounced off a brown Pontiac Trans Am on the left, then slid back into its lane.

As quickly as it had opened, the aiming space

was lost, and Katz and Manning were left fuming in frustration.

One of the terrorist hit men—suicidal to the end—refused to be spooked by the guns of Phoenix Force. He had a job to do. If it meant having his head turned into a blood-gushing sieve, he would do his job.

Leaning from the rear window, he coolly panned his M-16 across the side of the gasoline tanker in the left lane. The truck jockey was oblivious to the fact that his life was nearly over.

"Christ," Katz spit as he saw the enemy drawing his bead. "Dammit, McCarter, isn't there some way you can bull through there?"

"They won't budge," McCarter groaned, his face an acid-etched mask. "They've seen the guns. They're scared shitless." He fought to jam his way between a white Cadillac and a gold-toned Dodge, but the Caddy driver did not move. "Back off, you dumbass," he roared at the top of his lungs.

Finally, seeing Manning's rifle, the terrified man slowed cautiously. The Cadillac slid back fifteen feet. McCarter, drawing on all his driving skills, herded the big car into the slot and immediately nosed into the adjoining lane. He bluffed a frightened looking, middle-aged woman into giving way.

A long chute of highway suddenly appeared, and the Impala surged forward, engine rumbling, tires squealing. "Hot stuff, coming through," McCarter yelled.

Still, they were four car lengths behind the IRA

death wagon; when the tanker went up, they would be incinerated along with it. "Open up, Gary," Katz commanded. "Distract them any way you can."

Manning spied an opening and released a dozen more rounds, trying for a hit on the Toronado's gas tank. But his aim was faulty and the slugs tore out a Buick Skylark's right front tire, sending it into a crazy wobble, its driver banking into a pickup truck on his right. Brakes clamped, rubber shrieked, drivers cursed in sheer terror.

Phoenix Force was more hopelessly boxed in than before.

"Hellfire," McCarter raged. "We're dead for sure." He took a last desperate chance, flooring the accelerator, rocketing the Chevy back to the right at an even fifty-five, caromed off a compact Horizon and found fresh elbowroom. They continued running neck-and-neck with the gasoline tanker.

Slamming a fresh magazine into his weapon, Manning thrust himself farther out of the window, his hips braced precariously on the sill. He fought for a firing angle over the top of the car ahead of them. "Keio," he rasped. "Grab my legs." On the right side, Encizo was trying the same thing. Ohara clamped each man's thigh and hung on for dear life. The rapid-fire hammering of the CAR-15 and the Stoner M-63 boomed back inside the close confines of the car with near-concussive impact. Caught between the double onslaught, Keio winced in pain.

McCarter fought to break out of the trap, to escape the maze of slewing, screeching steel before Redfern and his thugs blew the top off the world. Deliberately he rammed a Volkswagen Rabbit, collapsing its side like some berserk demolition-derby driver. He exulted as the car slid right and locked with a Datsun behind it, clearing a slight opening.

Instantly McCarter banged into the hole, bullied a second driver into giving way. He roared as the Impala surged out, gained two car lengths and began to lead the tanker.

Manning and Rafael were forced to hold their fire, their free hands clawing for hold on the Impala's structure as McCarter maneuvered the vehicle.

The IRA killer made his move.

But the murdering bastard was not satisfied just to torch the tanker; he was determined to double the ante, kill a heady quota of those whom the firefall would never reach. The madman—still in cocky profile, as if daring Phoenix Force to stop him—deliberately stitched the cab with a half-dozen rounds, chopping the driver into ground round.

Then, assured that the runaway truck would wander across the freeway and cause a long back-up of maiming, deathdealing carnage, he emptied the rest of his magazine into the gasoline compartments.

In that frozen millisecond Manning and Rafael saw the perforations crawl across the tanks, gasoline gushing instantly, ignition delayed. Follow-up rounds, chipping at steel in relentless fury, provided the necessary sparks.

Rafael's gaze was torn in a dozen different directions, the enormity of the IRA brutality stunning him. It was too late, but he got the Stoner under control and sent the Irish death merchant to hell.

One moment the bastard was spraying the tanker, his lips curved in black hatred, the next moment the 5.56mm slugs literally sliced his head from his shoulders. The bloody skull sailed into the air, looping high, bouncing off the roof of a flame-swept Volvo, scuttling in gory trail on the asphalt.

Encizo was readjusting, trying for another attempt on the Toronado, when the sky-splitting blast erupted.

It was only because McCarter, in supreme reflex, gunned the Impala to seventy at that moment that Encizo and Manning did not join the enemy on the road. The sudden heat, the ear-splitting *whoomp* of the explosion jolted them savagely, tilting the car. The reverse current of the flashback emptied their lungs, all but sucking them from the windows.

"Santa Maria," Rafael gasped when at last he could breathe again. *Mother of God. Pray for us sinners, now and at the hour of our death.* The childhood prayer came to him.

His eyes bulged as he saw engulfing sheets of flame jet upward and sideways like a monstrous flamethrower, the truck disintegrating behind him. Raw gasoline inundated automobiles closest to the tanker, extinguishing already roaring flames, then bursting into a glass-exploding, steel-melting inferno all over again.

Fifty thousand gallons of gasoline were sluiced over the landscape, turning Interstate 5 into a lake of wildly burning flames. On the low edge of the freeway, the gasoline overran the shoulder, formed a waterfall of fire that cascaded down the incline and threatened the service road below. Instantly the tarmac became a vast stadium of roaring fire.

Cars, pickups, what was left of the huge carrier, all swerved and slid across the freeway like a slow-motion jumble of toys—spinning, colliding, bouncing away, colliding again.

As far as the eye could see, the hungry, licking flames raged, turning tires into hoops of fire, invading the imploded windows, turning the occupants of the cars into screaming, human torches.

In that split second, the members of Phoenix Force saw cars jar to a stop; they saw doors swing open; they watched in near-nausea as flame-covered bodies fell out. Some staggered upright and ran blindly into the blazing, grinding maw of death.

Cars, their gas tanks cooked to flash point, began to explode. The heat intensified with incredible speed. The fire then began leaping backward, from car to car, to where the nation's largest junk-yard was in the process of being formed.

It was all instantaneous, kaleidoscopic, bloody cameos that would be engraved on Phoenix Force's memories forever.

Finally, the rolling, greasy smoke mercifully blotted out the rest of the ghastly horror.

Katzenelenbogen shouted instructions to McCarter. "Keep this crate rolling!" His eyes went stony as he tried to rid his mind of the horror behind them. "We've got to get that IRA scum. We owe it to the innocents who've died." His voice took on an unearthly tone. "Get them. Don't lose them now. I *want* those bastards."

The vengeful words, the cold-blooded loathing in his voice fired up his men anew. The hatred became virulent, contagious.

Turning their backs on the holocaust behind them, they focused their hard, unrelenting gaze on the battered Toronado racing ahead, scurrying to lose itself in the glut of distant traffic. Each man tended to his weapons, replacing magazines in assault rifles, in automatics, slamming rounds into eagerly waiting chambers.

Vengeance, their hearts boomed.

Inside the Toronado it was time for fear. Of the six IRA hardmen who had started the barbaric joyride, only three were still alive. Denny Green, on the driver's extreme right, would never know the rich taste of Irish whiskey again. Slumped forward on the seat, his face all but gone, he bled the last of his life juices onto the floor, turning the mats slippery with gore. Tom Harker, jammed next to him, fought dizzying nausea—intermixed with chilling terror—and tried edging away from his dead comrade. Each time he did, the driver cursed him roundly, slamming a vicious elbow into his ribs.

In the back seat, only Pat Connor was still breathing. To his right, Paul Lannon, victim of Gary Manning's first burst, was collapsed like a rag doll, half on the seat, half on the floor. Connor at least had revulsion room and put distance between himself and the mangled body.

The luxury of space was his only because Will Donnaugh, who had blasted the gasoline tanker, was no longer aboard. The instant his head had parted company with his shoulders, he had flopped forward, half-in and half-out of the car. His stomach churning, Connor had executed a quick wraparound to his legs, and Donnaugh had become a long, spinning streak of blood on the pavement.

"Get y'r nose out there, Pat!" Matt Redfern, the driver and hit-squad topman, growled. "Keep 'em away from us, damn you. They're closing in on us, lad. *Move it*."

But Pat Connor was done fighting for the day. Made ashen-faced by the insane turn of events, his spine had turned to mush. Eyes haunted, he stared straight ahead and gave no indication that he even heard the commands.

"Shoot, man," Redfern screamed again, frenzied himself because he could not do two tasks at once. "Kill the American scum. It's our only chance. Or is it dyin' you're wantin', you coward?'' He turned to the man squeezed between him and Denny Green, administered a similar tongue-lashing. ''Don't just sit, Tom,'' he railed. ''Get loose, damn you. Get some lead in the air. Help that quivering woman back there.''

Harker, a faint trace of dedication left, emerged from his trance and allowed himself to be goaded into action. Squirming free, he got one foot onto the seat, struggled to boost himself into the back seat. He hung halfway, clawing for balance, so he could bring his M-2 into play.

But by then it was altogether too late for retaliation; time had finally run out for the IRA butchers. Redfern was no match for McCarter when it came to driving. Even as he closed in on the pack of vehicles running ahead of them, McCarter came alongside and viciously broadsided the Toronado.

The impact flung the teetering Harker back into the front seat, where he fell over Redfern, causing him to lose control of the Toronado. In that confused split second, McCarter deftly plastered his vehicle to the Toronado's right side. At the same time he swerved hard to the left, digging in just ahead of Redfern's bumper. Instantly the Toronado headed for the shoulder and guardrail on the freeway's high side, leaving Redfern no recourse but to slam his brakes to keep from going over.

It was eyeball-to-eyeball then; Manning could have reached into the IRA death wagon and gone at it hand to hand. His fingers screamed to pull the trigger at that close range, to send the terrorists to hell.

"Alive," Katzenelenbogen barked. "Get them alive. We can at least get some information out of them before we put them away. Hard cover, Gary. Blast them only if they move on you."

Again the Israeli was cheated. As the two automobiles screamed and shuddered to a stop, Redfern and Harker flung open their doors and bailed out. Foolishly emerging from his coward's coma, Pat Connor dazedly decided to protect himself. He brought up a languid right hand, tried to squeeze the trigger of a German P-38. Manning dispatched him with a point-blank, triple blast of 5.56mm slugs that opened Connor's face like an overripe squash.

Then there were two.

The Stoner roared.

Keio, unleashed for the first time, poured a quick dozen M-16 rounds across the Toronado's hood. Katz's Uzi spit death. The air was instantly clouded with smoke, redolent of cordite and scorched gun oil.

Suddenly the weapons went silent; there was an ominous hush. All that could be heard was the sound of two passing automobiles, freak survivors of the firestorm behind them. Gawking at the armed, crouching men, they limped past and headed for safety.

"Heads up, you bastards," Encizo called to the remaining IRA troops. "You've still got a chance. Throw out your weapons, come up with your hands high." As he spoke, the Cuban felt a decided itch in his trigger finger; he could almost feel the jarring impact in his shoulder as he envisioned himself obliterating an Irish face with a slashing haymaker.

"Stick it, Yanks," came the derisive retort, the voice heavy with an Irish brogue.

Keio made move to skulk behind the Impala, to test the IRA blind side, but Katz stalled him. "No risks," he hissed. "We can wait them out." He cast a quick glance out onto the freeway. "But not for long. Another five minutes and the area will be swarming with police.

"You've got ten seconds," Katz called over. "Then we're coming after you. You don't stand a chance of surviving."

For an answer there was staccato rapid fire from an automatic, the sound of tearing car steel, of shattering glass. "Try it, heroes," the defiant taunt carried. "We're waiting for you. You'll go with us, that's a damn fact."

"Hell," Katzenelenbogen cursed, "we can't wait all day. We'll blow our cover." He gestured to Keio. "A blast under the cars. Kneecap them."

Keio poked the M-16 under the Impala, adjusted. It roared a dozen times, was jerked back and steadied to receive a fresh magazine. There was a flurry of return fire, most of it wild, especially from the M-2, whose owner now rolled in agony, the lower part of his legs all but shot away.

He was still emptying the assault rifle in a crazy, skyward trajectory as Phoenix Force launched a two-pronged sweep. His mouth wide, screaming in excruciating pain, Tom Harker flopped helplessly, his knees shattered, bloody stumps. He still tried for a last shot at the enemy.

Again, too late. A three-round burst by Keio made his body almost dance across the ground, and he was gone.

Redfern was missing. Pinned down as he and Harker had been, only seconds intervening between the kneecap barrage and Phoenix's charge, there had not been time for escape.

Two quick shots rang out. Rafael Encizo was flung back as one slug tore the Stoner from his grasp, the second whistling shrilly mere inches from his eyes. Instantly all members of Colonel John Phoenix's unique antiterrorist team hit the dirt, blasting at the lip of the freeway. They scuttled forward on their bellies, weapons poised, hearts hammering.

Again an ominous silence descended upon them. Each man was reluctant to be the first to poke his head over the edge of the steep incline. "He's getting away," Manning hissed.

"Not for long he isn't," McCarter said, lobbing a grenade high and wide over the freeway shoulder. The sharp, flat, firecracker report sliced the air.

Instantly there was a rush for the brink. Heads, weapons poked over the edge, eyes darting for sight of the wounded enemy leader.

To the death, Redfern was determined to take company to hell with him. Again he opened up, two handguns spitting hot lead in Phoenix Force's direction. The team hit the dirt, then warily rose to look for Redfern again.

Wounded badly, Redfern had dropped behind a knoll sixty feet below, the snout of a huge runoff culvert providing slapdash cover. "McCarter," Yakov snapped, "seconds."

Another grenade, held for a crucial extra moment before being released, arced through the air and bounced off the culvert. A two-second count, another ear-muddling whump and it flowered high and wide, death-seeking shrapnel slicing down.

Redfern's lifeblood leaked out of his battered body. The concussion flung him up and away from the culvert. Cut to ribbons, Redfern was game to the last and desperately sought to regain his footing. The Uzi and the M-16 sang a joint death song. Redfern went down for good.

"McCarter," Katz said quietly. "Go make sure."

His Browning Hi-Power at ready—14-round magazine freshly recharged—McCarter legged it down the incline, scattering gravel and dirt as he went. Reaching the dead Irishman, he stared down at him with contempt. Memory of the innocents who had died because of the terrorists flooded back.

In the fast-enshrouding gloom Redfern's face was gaunt, his eyes weary, haunted.

With a sudden coldness in the pit of his stomach, McCarter started back up the hill, his movements oddly sluggish. As he climbed, he knew a growing sense of desolation and wondered how long before their vendetta with terrorist scum would come to an end.

The self-defeating thoughts were swiftly aborted as he came topside and loped to the bogged-down Impala, where the rest of the crew waited for him. He squeezed behind the wheel, cranked up the car and gunned the engine to rock the Chevy free from the Toronado. The flashing blue lights of police cruisers, ambulances and rescue vehicles were appearing in the distance; time was short. Finally with a shearing, scraping lurch, the cars came apart, and the Impala bucked forward.

They paused to let a siren-shrieking cruiser go past—running the wrong way on the wide-open freeway—then sedately moved forward. They looked back one last time to where the gloomy dusk was ablaze, to where a thunderhead of oily, black smoke climbed a mile into the sky.

They eased out, the cop car paying them no heed. One of the lucky ones, the police surmised, if they gave them any thought at all; someone who, by freakish turn of luck, had escaped the grisly inferno of death.

As, indeed, Phoenix Force had.

2

Irish terrorists kill thirty-two in freeway disaster

Thirty-two people died and 58 were injured yesterday afternoon on the Interstate 5 when a tanker carrying 50 thousand gallons of gasoline exploded.

Originally believed to be an accident, authorities have confirmed the explosion was deliberately set off by terrorists.

A spokesman for the Irish National Liberation Army (INLA), dissident arm of the Irish Republican Army (IRA), contacted the *Seattle Post-Intelligencer* offices yesterday evening, claiming responsibility for the attack, and saying it was the beginning of an all-out campaign against the United States. He said the attacks would continue until Washington comes to terms with the "Irish problem."

Witnesses of the disaster say the terrorists fired multiple rounds into the tanker, igniting the cargo. The truck driver lost control of the vehicle, causing 125 additional collisions as cars piled up on the busy freeway.

biles closest to the vehicle also fired up in flames, killing nearly all occupants.

"We have struck our first blow against the United States," the caller stated. "America must recognize the validity of the Irish cause or suffer the consequences. It (U.S.) has been toadying bootlickers to the British for too long. You will be hearing from Grey Dog again."

Grey Dog is apparently another faction of the INLA.

Police efforts to develop leads on the terrorist group have been unsuccessful. Police are also investigating reports by witnesses that the INLA vehicle was pursued by another vehicle. The search for the second team continues.

"We will exercise every effort to identify these cold-blooded murderers, to root out their confederates and bring them to swift justice," said J. Malcolm Haverhill, Chief, Defense Security Assistance Agency. "We will show the world that the United States will not tolerate such terrorist attacks on our soil. Furthermore, we shall...."

"In a pig's eye you will," McCarter exploded, tossing the newspaper aside. "You're not going to show the world anything—*we* will."

"What the hell?" Rafael Encizo soothed, a mocking smile on his face. "Who rattled your cage, *compadre*? Save it for the enemy."

"Up yours," McCarter growled. His growl then gave way to a grin.

Across the room sprawled on the bed, Keio Ohara smiled. "Nobody in their right mind rattles McCarter's cage."

Hal Brognola, leaning against the east wall, an open briefcase balanced on his lap, glanced to where Colonel Yakov Katzenelenbogen sat. "Any of these guys belong to you?"

"All of them," Yakov said softly, an unmistakable glint of pride in his eyes.

The night before, David McCarter had been drinking—not his usual quantity of Coke. Scotch. Neat. Gary Manning had at last persuaded him to drop a few ice cubes into the volatile stuff.

McCarter had never been much of a drinker, and about ten-thirty he had finally passed out. The members of Phoenix Force had breathed a sigh of relief, for he had become mean with the booze. None of his buddies had wanted to be the one chosen to try decking the drunk Brit.

By that time, Brognola had already been airborne, on his way west from Stony Man.

As they had waited for Brognola, McCarter had struggled up from a deep sleep. He had immediately started a ruckus upon finding his fifth of J&B missing. They had calmed him, coaxing a few cups of black coffee down his throat.

Things had been looking up. At least until McCarter had picked up the *Seattle Post-Intelligencer* and had begun reading the account of the tragedy. It was old news at best; the rest had caught the late-breaking reports on the TV news the night before.

Now, as Manning pushed a freshly prepared batch of eggs and sausage at him, McCarter's mouth was otherwise engaged. Manning persuaded him to drink a little milk, instead of the Coke he had asked for.

"What's this Grey Dog crap?" McCarter growled, not the least cowed at Brognola's presence. Or that of Clark Jessup, an irritating interloper, just introduced as the Phoenix Force-White House liaison. He, apparently, would be their pointman from here on in—whichever way the Irish donkey slashed its tail. Given total U.S. military and intelligence support, they would, hopefully, knot it in very short order. "I thought we were fighting the IRA." McCarter stonily stared at Jessup as though awaiting an explanation.

Jessup took in the unshaven, brawny six-footer, seated at the table in his T-shirt. The pencil pusher was definitely ill at ease.

These were the brutes he would be working with from now on?

This British hoodlum. The rangy Japanese with the cold, hooded eyes. The stocky Cuban who looked as if he could kill with his bare hands. The stolid, hard-faced Canadian who spoke only when absolutely necessary. The retread Israeli, who, with a steel hook where his right hand should be, struck the greatest terror of all into him. . . .

What kind of control could he hope to exercise over men like these?

None, if Phoenix had its way.

"What's this Grey Dog crap?" McCarter repeated. "They're goddamned amateurs." He scowled as he sopped up egg yolk with a scrap of toast.

"They're the worst kind," Manning interjected. "They have no concept of the odds against them. Nor do they care."

Brognola turned to the liaison man. "Any intelligence yet on how the IRA's taking this? Think they knew it was coming off beforehand?"

"It's highly unlikely that they didn't have some wind of it," Jessup replied in his precise, studied way. "But I doubt that they knew exact details, deadlines, the like. If they had they would have tried to forestall them in no uncertain terms.

"I expect they're screaming bloody murder at the moment. The U.S. has always been off limits to Irish terrorist attempts; there's too much American money and arms at stake. The IRA cause is very popular among certain segments of our population."

"But what's behind it?" Keio Ohara said, rising from the bed, the M-2 he had been studying still in his hands. "It has got to be something big for them to expose themselves like this...to murder innocent children and women the way they did."

"Swine," McCarter spit, a lifelong animosity for the Irish festering. "That's what the yellowbacks do best. Kill women and children."

"I think we all know what's behind it," Brognola broke in, definite "take-charge" in his manner. "The game plan's basically the same as when we first sent you out here. I think what happened yesterday was a fluke, a stupid miscue on INLA's part. Apparently they thought you guys were closing in, and they got a bit hysterical. They decided to play it by ear, to take some bodies with them when they checked out. You know the rest."

"And the bottom line?" Katzenelenbogen interrupted, an edge to his words.

"Oil," Brognola said. "You think we're the only ones who know that the Arabs are about to drop the other shoe. . . again? I'm sure every terrorist outfit in the world is in on that privileged information—and I'll bet they're working on an angle to use it to their best advantage. A new, worldwide oil embargo is definitely in the cards. I mean, *shutdown*. Today? Tomorrow? OPEC isn't saying. But it will come. And when it does it will shove the world into an economic abyss. If you think the Russians have us by the throat now, wait till then. We'll be playing kiss-ass with the Arabs like you wouldn't believe."

"So?" Encizo said. "Where do these INLA creeps fit into the picture?"

Relying on the vast intelligence that Mack Bolan and his Stony Man network had gathered over the past few months, Hal Brognola patiently briefed Colonel John Phoenix's satellite strike force on the over-all implications of the impending oil embargo. He carefully explained how the Irish National Liberation Army—via the hotheaded splinter faction operating as Grey Dog—hoped to capitalize on the world crisis, bend it to its own purposes. He emphasized Phoenix Force's part in quashing the INLA program before it got off the ground.

According to Stony Man's assessment, the IRA—the Provos, the Sinn Fein, the IRSP, the Ulster Red Hands, the INLA, Grey Dog and various other oddball groups cloaked in the general home-rule movement—had lately fallen upon hard times. They had suffered a general loss of momentum and a loss of prestige internationally—especially after the vicious bombing of the Royal Horse Guard in London in August 1982. While Castro, Khaddafi, and certain Marxist terrorist outfits in Europe continued sporadic support of the IRA cause with funds and smuggled weapons, American sympathy had waned since 1977. The terrorists were truly hurting.

The real crusher had been the Falkland Islands engagement between British and Argentine forces in early 1982. To the home-rule advocates it had become yet another example of British ruthlessness and high-handed imperialism. Worse had been the wholesale support given the U.K. by the Reagan administration, by the American populace itself. To these front-line terrorists it had become handwriting on the wall: their cause was doomed if they did not demonstrate dramatic aggression, elicit more worldwide support for the holiness of their cause.

In the case of Grey Dog, the message carried

even more clearly: make America pay for its indifference, for its rejection of their cause.

And, America paid in Seattle, Washington.

"Which brings us back to square one," Brognola said, "the over-all INLA strategy. What, exactly, are they up to? Where do they strike next?"

"Apparently," Katz mused, "they came to Seattle for one purpose, to blow up the oil-transfer terminals. Seattle's a crucial link in the Alaskan oil picture, as you well know. Knock out these facilities, and you put a kink in the overseas and national distribution program. Only we mopped up on them too soon. We were supposed to catch them in the act." He glanced to Brognola. "Sorry about that, Hal."

"Yakov," Brognola reassured, "it wasn't your boys who overreacted. *You* didn't shoot up that tanker. But you sure as hell took care of the guys who did."

"Our pleasure," McCarter said. "I'm only sorry we couldn't drag it out a bit, make those murdering bastards pay by inches."

Manning put the conversation back on track. "If we're to assume that the terrorists won't risk another hit at the docks because of beefed-up security, then we'd best assume that now they'll shoot for higher stakes." His mouth drew to a grim line. "Alaska itself. The Trans-Alaska Pipeline. They intend to bring America to its knees one way or another."

"That will be the day," Keio Ohara said with

surprising vehemence. "Not if I . . . we have anything to say about it."

"Christ," Encizo exclaimed, "that'll be a killer. If they blast the pipeline, our military and industrial potential will go down the tube. We'll have to put rubber bands in every car and truck in America."

"I can't realistically see these Grey Dog people attacking in Alaska," Clark Jessup inserted. "Not in the dead of winter. The weather there is impossible. Setting up a sabotage network at this time is highly improbable. If, indeed, that is their intent. You do tend to overdramatize at times, Mr. Brognola."

"Overdramatize?" Hal snarled. "Did that thing on the freeway sound like overdramatizing? Those bastards aren't here for the Christmas caroling, that's for sure. Even if they don't hit the pipeline, that doesn't mean they'll pull a cocoon act for the winter. They'll keep raising hell up and down the coastline until it's time for the main strike, or I miss my bet."

Katz looked hard at Brognola, inhaling his input. Then he asked the big Fed for a good game plan.

"For now we go on hold," Brognola said. "There'll be mop-up here, of course. We have to assume that there must be other INLA hardmen in the Seattle woodwork. If we can get a lead on a safehouse, or some such—"

"Negative on the reserves," Katz interrupted. "The six we killed, we had them staked out for three days. They never had any visitors, nor did they go anywhere other than on their harbor-area patrols. Keio bugged the phones in their rooming house. No incoming or outgoing calls."

"A self-contained cell then," Brognola said grudgingly. "Though it seems highly unlikely. There have to be others in the area. It's inconceivable they'd leave a mission like this to so small a cadre." He shrugged. "Our intelligence net will keep us posted in any event. When something breaks you'll know it."

"How many terrorists do you estimate?" Katz asked.

"At least fifty. Stony Man has no hard info on that, however. Hell, if they slipped out underneath the very noses of the Provos.... The INLA membership is up. Possibly two hundred all told. Since the old timers have laid back, the firebrand types have been flocking their way."

"Do you suppose they've already gone to Alaska?" Manning ventured. "Maybe the main force has been there right along. This Seattle mess could just have been a feint."

"Well," said Brognola, "if that's the case, they'll find a welcoming committee. The military, the TAP officials have been alerted of possible sabotage. They'll have security at peak, that's certain."

"But eight hundred miles of pipe?" McCarter scoffed. "How are you gonna watch all that?"

Brognola and Jessup spread various files and topographical charts across the grubby, oilcloth-covered tabletop. For the next hour the seven men pored over the reports, studied pipeline schematics. Main pumping stations, receiving stations, bridges, mainline gate valves, the vast tank farm terminal at Valdez, containment dikes and tanker berths, the computer microwave control centers— all came under scrutiny as possible INLA targets. Which link could be attacked with least casualty risk?

"Jesus H. Christ," McCarter groaned, midway through the session. "It's like finding a needle in a haystack. They can hit us in a thousand different places."

"Not all at once," Yakov smiled. "Remember, there are only fifty or so of them. Doesn't that make you feel much better?"

"Not that you'd notice." He paused, came back with a new avenue of conjecture. "Just who in hell's backing these bleedin' bastards, anyway?"

"I'd put it at the doorstep of one of the Saudi sheikhs," Brognola said. "A couple million here, a couple million there. Who's to miss it? The INLA has it both ways. They settle a score with the U.S., and clear a dandy little profit besides. If they ever return to the Emerald Isle alive, that is."

Brognola went on to detail the snowballing profits to the OPEC nations that the destruction of the TAP could bring. It would take at least six months to repair the damage the INLA strike force could inflict. If OPEC was to declare a shutdown immediately upon crippling the Alaska pipeline, American reserves would be depleted within forty days. After that it would be all gravy—the sky, pricewise, would be the limit.

"And the sheikhs *will* enforce it," Brognola stressed. "No cut rating by marginal oil-producing nations this time. I wouldn't doubt they've already got terrorist groups lined up all over the globe, each cell waiting for the first hint of embargo violation. They'll blow that tanker, the tanker berth off the face of the earth in a minute flat. Just one incident like that and no oil would move anywhere. The world would come to terms, or else.

"I'd bet any kind of money that there are Irish enforcers already on retainer, just waiting for someone to blow that first whistle. Not INLA, but other Irish terrorists. A spin-off, a bonus, sort of, for INLA's larger part in their whole scheme. The rotten bastards."

"Lovely world we live in, eh, mate?" McCarter muttered.

"Names, Hal?" Katzenelenbogen asked, falling back in his chair, the curved prongs of his prosthetic device clicking nonstop, as they always did when he was perturbed. "Who are we fighting, anyway?"

"Names, yes. But confirmation? No. The INLA leadership's been seesawing ever since Seamus Costello was wiped out in a gang assassination back in 1977. They don't exactly publicize their latest topcock. He wouldn't come stateside anyway. They'd send a second- or third-in-command. So far we've got a guy named Sean

Toolan, another called Bryan Cafferty. Which is boss man? Your guess is as good as mine. Oh, yes. One other, a Collie Devane, but we have just a name on him, nothing more. This Toolan character is one tough hombre, we hear, a paranoid type who kills for the sake of killing.''

"You just made my day," Yakov said.

A short time later Hal Brognola called the briefing to a close. But there was a final adjuration after Clark Jessup had already excused himself and left the room.

"The item in the news about an 'opposing force' that was observed yesterday. It couldn't be helped, considering the circumstances. On behalf of Colonel Phoenix I must remind you that, no matter what, your identity must never be revealed; that is foremost in our over-all program. Should the press ever get hold of names and descriptions, our effectiveness would be destroyed.''

His jaw went taut, the cords in his throat became prominent. "Do I make myself clear?"

To a man Phoenix Force nodded silently.

"You guys...and Able Team...and Mack, of course...are the last hope of a world that is on the verge of being flushed down the tube. You cannot fail. Because if you do, our country's last, gasping breath will likewise be snuffed out. So remember how sacred a mission yours is.''

He spoke very slowly now, his voice emotional. "Know of Mack Bolan's respect for you, his pride in your work, his...love and gratitude for the fact that you're willing to lay your lives on the line for him, for his cause.''

Then he was gone.

Afterward it seemed the silence would last forever, each man deeply lost in his thoughts.

It was Keio Ohara who breached the impasse. Turning away abruptly, he returned to the M-2 he had been tinkering with and began dismantling it.

As if mesmerized, the others watched Keio fieldstrip the weapon he had liberated from Tom Harker's grasp. Shortly they were assisting, advising him when the components did not readily disengage. They marveled at the pride of workmanship exhibited in its knurled handgrip, the walnut trigger handle, in the careful, precise machining. They lamented the fact that, due to pettifogging politics over caliber variance, the gun had never gone into mass production.

"Wonder where that Paddy got it," McCarter said, minor awe in his voice. "A damned museum piece is what it is. I'd wrap the bloody thing up, send it home to my mum if it was mine."

For the moment the serious words of Hal Brognola—the weight of the holy trust he had just laid upon them—were forgotten. Almost eagerly the men allowed themselves to become engrossed in the beauty of the captured assault rifle. It became a convenient way to wriggle free from the sense of impending doom. Once again they lost themselves in the business at hand.

In the business of war.

The business of death.

3

Christmas Eve on a U.S. Army base is pure hell.

Bad enough to be stuck in camp at the festive time in a stateside military installation. But to be isolated in the fierce winter of Alaska—at Fort Greely in particular—that is piling misery atop misery.

It was 1400 hours, and already the base was almost entirely deserted. Everyone who could wangle a pass for the holidays had checked out shortly after noon, heading for Anchorage, Fairbanks, even the Yukon. Action of any sort was better than sitting in camp watching frostbitten fingers fall off one by one. Booze, bright lights, girls, even a good fistfight was preferable to slow suffocation at Big Delta.

Such were the thoughts of PFC Eddie Gorman as he sullenly marched guard duty, his post encompassing the modest ordnance buildings the base boasted. It was a half-mile tour around the six-foot-high fence surrounding the three cement-block buildings, and though the weather was mild—an even zero—the wind was harsh and cutting.

Gorman wore the regulation one-piece, white,

down-lined winter issue and carried an M-16, muzzle down, on his shoulder. His feet were clad in boots that were developed during the Korean campaign, and protected to eighty degrees below zero. Even with his parka pulled snug, the long fur already iced from breath vapor, the chill still managed to work through.

Perhaps it was not so much cold as it was nostalgia that gripped Gorman most. In truth, it was his first Christmas away from home, and he was homesick. The Sony Walkman secreted inside his hood, drawing plaintive Christmas carols from a Fairbanks FM station, did little to help. Listening to music while on guard was definitely verboten, but Gorman risked it. *Screw them,* he thought. *If they can shove me out in the snow, turn down my pass request on Christmas Eve, the least they can do is allow me music while I walk my post.*

Even more galling, he thought, was the pointlessness of the duty. What was he guarding? Who was going to bother Uncle Sam's lousy, two-bit guns on Christmas Eve?

And should anyone decide to seize the crap, what good would he and his backup, Mungo Harris—they were spelling each other, two on, two off—do? Before he could activate his two-way, secure help, the enemy would be long gone. The men inside the armory, he was sure, would offer no resistance to speak of.

Even if he got out a Mayday, Gorman snorted, who would respond? The camp was an absolute ghost town.

There were lights inside the ordnance buildings, bright pinpricks in the murk, where a skeleton crew—fifteen to twenty men at best—had pulled special duty. Also denied holiday liberty, they were involved in round-the-clock repair and maintenance in preparation for upcoming field exercises scheduled for mid-January.

Suckers, Eddie Gorman gibed inwardly. Welcome to the club.

His Sony served up "White Christmas," and he was stabbed with sadness. His bitterness returned. They could have *this* white Christmas, he thought. *What I should be guarding is Betty, over in Fairbanks. Sure as hell she'll get all bitter-ass over my being confined to base on Christmas.*

Though it was now 1415 hours it might as well have been dusk. Or dawn—it was all the same. Either way, visibility was almost nil. The Alaskan winter solstice upon them, the sun had sunk beneath the horizon for good a few days ago; it would not poke up its rosy-red face for two weeks.

Caught in the craggy embrace of the Alaska mountain range to the south, the eternal twilight became ever darker at Fort Greely. The mere act of lighting up a cigarette, another no-no, which Eddie blithely flaunted, came on like a minor flash fire, the lighter flame almost blinding in the depressing gloom.

There had been a smattering of milky light to the south at noon. Things had gone downhill since then.

Staring through the vapor-frosted window his

parka provided, Gorman could see no landmarks beyond two hundred yards. A fog that was not a fog. The eerie half-light turned everything flat, made outlines vague. The C Company barracks in the next block were dim, indefinite blobs, even the window lights somehow watery, faded. The mountains themselves were amorphous, a smudge more than anything else. Had he not known where Mount Hayes was, he easily could have mistaken the brooding mass for a low-hanging cloud.

Abruptly Gorman faltered in mid-stride as he heard a helicopter, swinging in swiftly at ten o'clock. He searched the murk for its running lights and was puzzled when he saw none. There had been another, flying low, at 1300 hours, just as he had come on duty.

He was not unduly alarmed. In the Arctic, aircraft were commonplace at any time of day or night, and in winter choppers and ski planes were the main mode of transportation.

But when the whirlybird executed a wide turn, dropped to five hundred feet, began circling the ordnance shops and angling for the abbreviated motor-pool area just behind the fence a hundred yards at a jump, he was alerted. They were going to land.

Momentarily the nineteen-year-old kid froze, panic jamming up into his throat like a fist. He fumbled for his walkie-talkie, feverishly thumbed the transmit button.

"Hey, Mungo," he blurted, ignoring radio procedure, "get your ass over here. Get the C.O., tell him somebody's landing a chopper in the motor pool. It looks like a raid or something. Mungo, do you read me?''

Huge, billowing clouds of powder snow churned up in a small blizzard as the phantom copter adjusted and carefully began settling down in front of the eighteen-foot loading doors at building one. As it neared touchdown, the doors slammed open on both sides; dark garbed figures dropped into the snow and charged toward the building. As the snow calmed somewhat, Gorman could see their assault rifles at ready, the muzzle-flashes watery orange, the reports partially muffled by the growl of the idling chopper.

''Hey,'' he called, reacting in stupid, childlike reflex. ''Halt. Identify yourselves.'' When the attack force ignored him, he snapped off the safety on his M-16 and slapped in a magazine containing six rounds. ''Halt. Do you hear?'' Terror closing his throat, he touched off two slugs in the single-round mode.

As the tumblers screamed through the air, splatted off a concrete wall, the intruders took heed. Instantly two of the enemy spun in their tracks and sent a half-dozen rounds each in Gorman's direction. Two 7.62mm projectiles smashed into Eddie's chest, turned his heart and lungs to chopped meat and exited through his back, leaving a hole as big as a cantaloupe.

The fuzzy-cheeked kid flopped backward, his hands high. He dropped with a thump, his head cracking on the roadway. He spasmed once, twice and died.

Kneeling to the right of the copter, about fifty feet from the armory door, the INLA leader tugged down the hood of the camouflage-design parka, fighting the rotor backwash. "Back, men," the voice snarled. "Give Martin room to blow that door."

Inside the building heads began bobbing up in the windows, the work crews inside curious about the commotion. An AK-47 and a Sten Mark 6 casually took out the glass, mangled an American soldier's head. The other rubberneckers instantly dropped out of sight.

Martin, the demolitions expert, did his job. Twenty seconds later the plastic explosives detonated. It was a small charge, the muffled roar not carrying any farther than three hundred yards. The door collapsed inward, small sheets of flame licking upward.

"Let's get 'em," Sean Toolan bellowed, his fearlessness infectious. "Clean out the Yank bastards." His Sten stuttered, the high-velocity rounds tearing a second door to tatters, killing anyone unlucky enough to be standing behind it.

"Fast about it," Toolan's second-in-command barked. "Before the Americans can gather their bloody wits. In the name of sweet Jesus, Flaherty. Will you move your fat, girlish ass!"

The eight-man team charged forward as one, Toolan leading the attack through the small door, Collie Devane in the forefront as the rest poured through the gaping hole in the loading entrance.

An Army ten-ton truck was parked in the loading bay. To the right the gun compartments, protected with heavy steel doors, came into view. "Martin, me lad," Devane exhorted, "you've got your work cut out for you. Get to it. We'll go forward, do a bit of head-hunting."

With an impatient motion, Devane tossed back the hood of the constricting cold-weather jump suit. As the parka fell, a cloud of long, red hair burst free and was flung wildly to clear it from the fur lining. Large, luminous, green eyes, a thin, high-boned face, the slightest slash of lipstick at the cruel mouth revealed Devane to be a woman—a tough, hell-for-leather woman.

As she surged forward, the twenty-eight-year-old female railed at her troops anew. "Dammit, Rory—" she gave one sluggard a vicious shove "—will you be forever waiting for a woman to take the lead?" She brought up her AK-47, and Rory Swaine scurried on ahead. It was difficult to discern which he feared most: the unknown American strength before him, or the russet-haired firebrand behind.

A wide corridor, flanked by cubbyhole offices and spare-part storage areas, led into a vast repair room. In that room, large steel-sheeted workbenches, each shielded by steelplate partitions, took up one wall. A labyrinth of steel shelving—parts storage for armament in repair—stretched away at the far end. Here, partially protected by heavy steel of sorts, the six remaining GIs had chosen to make their stand.

There had been eight. But one now lay along the

west wall, drenched in blood from the direct hit he had taken. The other technician, finding expedience the better part of valor, had fled through a rear door, breaking for the distant ordnance shops to sound the alarm.

The remaining personnel had seized whatever operable weapons came to hand, carbines, M-1s, M-16s. Mostly they carried regulation issue .45 automatics. Ammo, because of the panicky, emergency situation, was in critically short supply, thus they wisely husbanded rounds.

As Devane, Flaherty and Swaine leapfrogged to where Toolan and Tom Lynch crouched behind a table, they were half deafened by the intermittent chatter of the Sten, of an M3A1, by the Yanks' return fire.

"We'll have to be quick about it, Coletta," Toolan called back to where she had dropped behind the wall forming the office area. He craned his neck cautiously and panned the tangle of high-standing storage bins with his Sten Mark 6. His nostrils flared with excitement, an eerie paranoid glitter in his eyes. He was impatient for a real bloodbath to begin. "The runner there, he'll be bringing help. Them boys we won't take by surprise. Martin, is he at it?"

"Listen for y'rself," Coletta Devane said with a supercilious smirk. At the moment a muffled blast carried from the rear of the building. "I imagine that should do it. Come on, Sean. Let these boys be. They're no match for us. . .they've got shit in their blood. They'll help us load up if we ask 'em nice. Time's running out, man.''

Toolan's lips drew back over his teeth, the bloodlust in his gaze absolutely blazing now. "No," he spit. "Dead is how we leave this scum. Payback for what the Yanks did to Redfern and the rest in Seattle." He chuckled. "A little calling card. To let them know we ain't gone yellow all at once." The Sten punched out three rounds to punctuate his meaning. A gurgled scream from the stacks testified to the accuracy of his aim.

Sean Toolan, in his mid-thirties, was definitely "black Irish." Compact and lean, standing five-ten, his eyes were dark, his skin ruddy, his hair coal black. There was a deceiving sensuousness in the full lips, in the evasive gaze, that hinted at vulnerability. It was these eyes—Toolan's "lost sheep" look—that particularly appealed to Coletta Devane and turned her to so much mush when they were alone together.

Toolan's jawline, ever set in tension, was prominent, his brows thick, craggy, providing a strong overhang to his piercing glare. His teeth clenched, a cruel grin forming. Then the man was up, darting to the right, his machine gun chattering, carrying the fight to the enemy.

"Move in," he roared, hitting the concrete, flopping onto his stomach, elbow-walking himself deeper into the storage-bin alleyways.

His sheer bravado thrilled Devane. Instantly she flung herself forward, taking the place Toolan had just deserted. She fired her AK-47 high into the opposite wall, a quick burst, hoping for the slugs to ricochet down into the GI rearguard.

The Americans opened up, pinning the Irish force down momentarily. In the gloom Coletta saw Toolan snaking his way along the far alley. She waved Flaherty up and simultaneously lunged to the left. She advanced twenty feet, then darted behind a wheeled trash dumpster. From the edge of the steel box she saw a GI in green fatigues at the end of his steel tunnel, eyes searching the shadows, his M-16 pointed in Sean Toolan's direction.

It was like shooting fish in a barrel. Devane tripped off a half-dozen rounds and took the man down, blood spurting like a miniature fountain from his back.

The attack was over in minutes.

The GIs, caught unawares and without adequate firepower, were no match for the case-hardened Grey Dogs. Tom Lynch took a hand. Inspired by Toolan, he literally ran the length of the room, pausing a moment at each opening in the bins, firing a quick burst of .45 slugs down each alley. Toolan, meanwhile, was providing a withering cross fire between the opening of two medium-height shelves.

Instant slaughter.

The sound of cursing groans, shrill screams built up immediately as Lynch completed his route. There was no more return fire from the Americans.

Breaking the silence of the American wipeout,

was a squeaky voice. "Please, you guys," it called, "no more. I give up. Take the stuff. Take anything you want. Only don't shoot anymore. Don't kill me...."

Toolan emerged from behind the first bin. "You," he commanded. "Throw out your weapon."

A Colt .45 automatic instantly sailed from the depths of the shelving and bounced off one of the workbenches.

"No tricks, you bastard," Toolan barked. "If you pull anything, we'll chop you up for dog meat. Come out with your hands clamped behind your head."

The GI could not have been more than twenty. He was blond, ashen-faced. Pure fear contorted his face; a betraying darkness stained his trousers where he had involuntarily emptied his bladder. When he saw the enemy, his eyes went runny; he blubbered. "Please. I don't wanna die...."

A contemptuous sneer on her lips, Coletta Devane advanced on the soldier, his Colt .45 now in her hand. "He's just a wet-nosed kid. He's gone and pissed his drawers." Her laughter was shrill, harsh.

"C'mon, Coletta," Toolan snapped. "Get on with it. Put him away."

"Must we, Sean?" she said softly, a sensual yearning clouding her gaze. "He's a good-looking lad. Tall, too. All things being in proportion, you know...."

"Christ, Coletta," Toolan barked. *"Do it."*

The GI, his fear beyond words, just stood there and shook.

Coletta raised the kid's gun. The .45 boomed a point-blank shot at his skull. The GI's head bucked back violently, the force of the slug straightening him, his arms flailing. A jet of blood and brain matter sluiced across the surface of a nearby workbench. The soldier dropped to his knees then pitched onto his face.

Devane turned, regarded Toolan contemptuously. She took pains tucking the gun into her belt. "You can be such a pain in the arse sometimes."

"Bitch," he spit, his voice a ridiculous croak.

At that moment the glass in the upper panes exploded, the sound of rapid fire carried clearly from outside. A thousand shards of glass rained down.

"The marines have landed," Coletta remarked, a strange flatness in her tone. Reflexively she ducked and ran in a low crouch toward the rear door, reloading her AK-47 as she went. The rifle began spitting fire the moment she kicked open the door.

"Lynch," Toolan called in staccato command, "you and Swaine get out that side door. Keep the bastards away from the helicopter. Get Cafferty outta the cockpit for backup if you have to."

Reluctant to miss out on the firefight, he sluggishly turned to the back of the building. "You, Flaherty. Help me and Martin load up."

The INLA vanguard was, however, in no serious jeopardy. The Fort Greely soldiers, still shell-shocked, incredulous over the terrorists' audacity, were not getting any closer to the action than was absolutely necessary. They peppered the terrorists listlessly, most of the shots wide. The cold, their half-dressed state and their confusion contributed to wholesale ineffectiveness.

One GI boldly advanced on the rear door in a zigzag run. Only one terrorist stood in his way. The GI's M-16 was swung down, the muzzle punching red holes into the thickening gloom.

But suddenly he felt as if someone had slammed him across the knees with a baseball bat. He screamed, crashed to the ground, flopped wildly. He continued shrieking, aware that his legs were gone.

In the doorway Coletta Devane giggled, lifted her AK and raised hell with a Jeep to her right, where another GI crouched.

In the weapons-storage compartments, Sean Toolan, smarting beneath the snide, sidelong looks Bernard Flaherty sent him from time to time, exorcised his resentment by working like a sweathog at the loading. He and Flaherty struggled with case upon case of M-16s, slamming them onto the helicopter deck at breakneck pace. Inside the chopper—a Bell XH-40, UH-1, a special heavy-duty "Huey" Model 214B built to lift 16,000 pounds—Marty Hoy and Bryan Cafferty strained mightily to keep up, shifting crates to equalize the load.

When they had loaded two hundred M-16s on

board, along with 20,000 rounds of ammo, they spread out to see what other military toys they might find. Two cases of Colt .45 automatics were loaded, along with a thousand rounds of ACP. Grenades, a couple of mortars and a hundred shells went on board almost as an afterthought. Two Browning .50s took Toolan's fancy, and they threw those in—with sufficient ammo—also.

Cold as it was, the men's faces were bathed with sweat by the time the last items were loaded.

Two minutes later, after a devastating eighteen-minute visit at Fort Greely, the Bell "Huey" was lifting off. The doors were open wide, two hard-men hanging out on each side, firing and picking off any GIs who tried to take a last shot at the lumbering aircraft.

The chopper swung sluggishly and headed due north. It gained altitude then leveled off. It was then swallowed up in the arctic twilight. The shapes below dissolved into watery nothingness.

Below, in the savaged ordnance building, the post constabulary was convening, but too late. They fought nausea and undermining terror as they appraised the swift slaughter the terrorist shock troops had so offhandedly inflicted.

4

"Welcome to the Twilight Zone," McCarter muttered as he stared down from the cockpit of the Bell 206L Long Ranger that Clark Jessup had requisitioned through civilian sources. Though they cruised at snail's pace, hovering a scant fifty feet above the tortuous snake that was the Trans-Alaska Pipeline, visibility was poor.

"And isn't it a pretty sight?" McCarter added.

"What you can see of it," Keio Ohara said. "Which is not very much."

It was a fair appraisal, for conditions were even worse than at Fort Greely. The farther north they went, the darker the days got. It was eternal night, the stars twinkling around the clock.

"I can see more than this when I'm in scuba gear," Encizo, their underwater expert, said. "Sixty feet down. In a river."

Gary Manning offered no comment, maintaining his hunched-over pose, his eyes fixed on the dim outlines of the forty-eight-inch pipe beneath them. The gray snake floated in graceful curves over the flattest of terrain; it traversed a frozen river on an ingeniously designed bridge, and in other spots it went underground to avoid blocking centuries-old migration pathways of caribou and reindeer.

Ahead, in vague configuration, lay a back-and-forth arrangement resembling a badly gapped zipper. As with all the surface layouts viewed thus far, the fish-trap pattern here rode on steel vertical support members (VSMs,) the pipe clamped into Teflon "shoes" that allowed it to flex and slide, thus providing for thermal contraction and expansion, for the frequent and severe quakes Alaska takes for granted.

Like the others, Gary Manning was frustrated by the short-range visibility. And they were supposed to find the Irish terrorists in this, he thought. It was like trying to see through Vaseline-coated wind goggles.

"Will someone adjust the contrast, please?" Rafael quipped.

It was December twenty-sixth, 1000 hours. Almost two days had passed since the Fort Greely massacre, and nothing more had been heard from the Irish National Liberation Army. Apparently they had gone to ground and would bide their time before striking again.

At that moment, according to calculations made by copter pilot Mitch Ransome, Phoenix Force was heading due south, crossing the North Slope, sixty-six miles from Prudhoe. It was at Prudhoe, after leaving Fort Greely, that they had spent what remained of Christmas in briefings at pumping station one, located on the edge of Prudhoe Bay, an extension of the Beaufort Sea.

Tomorrow, if things went according to schedule, they would have a grand tour of the Valdez shipping-and-receiving installation.

It would be, however, anticlimactic; they had already seen more than enough to boggle their minds.

Beneath them, stretching as far as the eye could see, was a virtual ocean of snow ribbed with constantly changing, blowing drifts. With the exception of the pipeline, there was no other indication of man's presence on a seemingly snowbound planet. The landscape awed the men of Phoenix Force, humbling them, nailing down the magnitude of their mission with crushing force.

A smudge on the southern horizon caught Encizo's eye. "What's that?" he asked Ransome, shouting to be heard above the roar of the engine and the clatter of the rotors.

"The Brooks mountain range, sir," Ransome replied. "Roughly eighty-five hundred feet high where we'll be crossing."

"God," McCarter exploded. "Will somebody turn on the goddamned lights?"

"We're north of the Arctic Circle here," Bill Davey, the copilot, offered, enjoying the discomfiture of their odd-lot charter. He had helped load their duffel at Prudhoe and had had opportunity to poke his fingers into the long, plastic-wrapped bags as he had stored their stuff aft. Men do not hunt caribou with assault rifles. "It won't brighten up for a while."

Neither fly-boy discounted the men's competence with the weapons. They were not green-horns. They would not tangle with these men for any kind of money—even the older gent with stainless steel where his right hand should be. He would take your eyes out with one quick swipe.

Outside it was twenty degrees below. With a mild wind-chill factor, the temperature easily fell to sixty-five below; exposed human flesh would freeze solid within a minute.

But inside the Bell 206L it was a toasty sixty degrees. The helicopter had capacity for greater warmth, but to its passengers, all bundled in winter gear—Phoenix Force in white, special Fort Greely issue—the heat was stifling. When the customers unzipped their jackets, the pilot's suspicions were further confirmed. Shoulder leather was visible everywhere. The cutthroat team was armed to the hilt.

"What do you think, Yakov?" Rafael spoke quietly, so the pilots would not hear. "We got any chance at all? How can we ever hope to head these bastards off at the pass?"

"Eight hundred miles," Katz mused. "Incredible. And we've got to guard that."

Gary Manning stuck his head into the huddle. "That complex at Prudhoe," he offered, "there's enough there alone to keep us busy for months. If you ask me, this blasted pipeline is indefensible."

"Absolutely," Yakov replied. "Maybe that's why the Irish chose the pipeline in the first place. They'll go for America's jugular. And with minimal risk." He smiled. "That's why they invited us in. The impossible will take a day extra."

"Destiny's darlings is what we are," McCarter mocked from over Manning's shoulder. "We get all the easy ones."

"If I was one of those Paddies," Rafael said, "I'd concentrate my efforts at Prudhoe. Cut off the oil at the source."

"Hitting Valdez wouldn't do the U.S. much good either," Keio Ohara joined in. "Just the same, I would plan to strike four or five critical spots at the same time."

"Perhaps that accounts for the lack of activity in the past forty-eight hours," Yakov observed. "That's probably what they're in the process of setting up. There will be multiple strikes, mark my words."

"They blow the TAP in a half-dozen places," said McCarter, "and everything stops automatically. The computers do it. But that still doesn't take out the oil already in the pipe. By the time they fix the holes, winter will have done its damnedest. Alaska will be proud owner of the biggest Chapstick in the world. They'll be six months cleaning out that shit."

"And America will be having a new love affair with the bicycle," Manning said.

"There are twelve pumping stations down there, fully housed and manned around the clock, more than any other pipeline in the world," Keio said, spitting back info the team had gleaned from yesterday's critique by the Sohio engineering staff.

"There are one hundred fifty-one control valves spaced along the Trans-Alaska Pipeline, seventy-one of them mainline valves. With targets like that, the Irish are probably running in circles deciding which to hit."

Recalling the tour of the vast complex at Prudhoe yesterday, each man stunned by the enormity of the process involved in pressuring raw crude into the pipeline, Katz repeated, "I'd say Prudhoe would be their first priority. The computer rooms, the heating areas, the refining and cutting plants, the initial flow operation, the generators.... It would take a billion dollars to rebuild that."

"But that's a high-profile site," Manning, Phoenix's engineer-in-residence, remarked. "There is security of sorts. Not security to my mind, but somebody must have been satisfied with the half-assed setup they got stuck with. No, I'd say they'll hit the TAP somewhere down the line. Maybe a strike on Prudhoe, but the main attack will come at one of the pumping stations, on the pipeline itself."

"Then," Katzenelenbogen said, "you'd say that the INLA would most likely be holed up in this very area."

"Perhaps. But I'd bet they'd light somewhere closer to the Brooks mountain range. There's more cover there." Manning surveyed the sea of snow beneath them. "Couldn't hide anything down there."

"But where in the mountains?" Rafael asked. "We quizzed the Prudhoe experts on that one. All the construction camps were dismantled or blown up, just to prevent that sort of thing.''

"Stands to reason they've got a base camp somewhere in this quadrant,'' Manning replied.

"But why set up a base?'' McCarter challenged. "Why not just zip in, do their dirty work and be gone? End of lesson.''

"Multiple strike,'' Gary Manning repeated emphatically. "That kind of thing takes time to set up. I wouldn't be surprised to find they already have a double agent on staff at Prudhoe. That last electrical engineer we met with yesterday, he didn't take to us that much. Fred Avancini, was it? I didn't like the look of him at all.''

"C'mon now, Gary,'' McCarter scoffed. "An inside man? Hell, this is just one of your everyday hit-and-run setups. Remember how clumsy they were in Seattle? The way they went into hysterics, just because we spooked 'em?''

"It's very possible,'' Manning insisted.

It was something to consider. And for the next ten minutes the men of Phoenix Force fell silent, mulling over the myriad options left to Sean Toolan, Bryan Cafferty, or whoever the Grey Dog top man was. The more they thought about the hopelessness of their mission, the more depressed they got.

Particularly preoccupied was Manning, who considered Alaska an extension of Canada proper, his native stomping grounds. To him the impending pipeline attack was dramatic testament to the growing terrorist contagion. If such an unlikely invader as the Irish National Liberation Army could strike Alaska, who then was safe? This new threat spurred, cemented his dedication to the new war.

It was a responsibility the taciturn, thirty-two-year-old security consultant lived with twenty-four hours a day. Indeed, his dedication to the cause had already cost him his marriage. A workaholic to start with, a perfectionist to boot, he had been a token husband to Lorraine almost from the start. Still, she had remained steadfast. But when Colonel John Phoenix had summoned him, his abrupt and secret departures from hearth and kin had written finis to what could have been a storybook romance.

Gary often thought of Lorraine. He envied her second marriage, the son she had given her new husband. He wondered if he could ever love another woman as much as he had loved her. At the same time he doubted that he would ever marry again. Why ruin another woman's life?

There were female relationships, to be sure. But he would be the first to admit that they were matters of convenience: companionship at times when he tired of his own company, a release of certain physical pressures, nothing more. Should any woman press for a more permanent commitment, it would mean a discreet goodbye.

He accepted his priorities squarely. It was a monasticism he could live with.

His needs were simple. The ruddy-faced, raw-boned man was a consummate woodsman, a jogging fanatic, a dilettante gambler and sports-car buff. His flourishing security-consultant career afforded him his collection of handguns, hunting rifles, Ferrari 308GTS and an occasional jaunt to Caribbean gambling haunts.

His hair the same tawny shade as McCarter's but worn close-cropped to his head, his body firm, lithe, yet decidedly muscular, Manning was considered handsome by those women who got past his blunt manner.

Looking down on the bleak, icy wastes of Alaska, Manning puzzled over the INLA impasse with an unflinching sense of reality. If the terrorists did not beat them, the merciless Arctic would; it was double jeopardy all the way. The slightest miscue could mean death for any or all of them. Again the quiet mood of dedication. He vowed he would hold up his end of things. If each Phoenix Force member did likewise, they would come through all right.

He looked about the cabin at the others and savored a private smile.

He would trust his life to any of them. He was positive that the feeling was mutual.

And, little by little, the tension in his gut eased.

Satisfied with what they had seen of the North Slope, Katz told the pilot to take the helicopter up and make for the mountains with all safe speed. As they cruised through an all-enshrouding ground fog, visibility worsened. The pilot, activating the radar and relying on "bush" instincts, carefully dropped beneath the clouds and picked his course by landmark sightings. He had flown in six times a day during construction of this leg of the pipeline; he knew the terrain like the back of his hand.

He pointed out where the pipeline ran—the main portion of it was buried in the rugged setting—and he indicated a vaguely defined pumping station. "That's Atigun Pass," he yelled over the engine racket. "It's the last of four stations on this side of the divide. It provides the final kick in the ass as the oil comes over the Atigun Saddle. It's the highest elevation point in the whole pipeline. Four thousand eight hundred feet."

"That's some layout," said Keio. "Looks like a whole village. Is all that necessary to pump oil?"

"You bet," Ransome replied. "Each station's got four, 13,500-horsepower gas turbine engines, three working, one on reserve. They put the crude—heated to a hundred-forty degrees to keep it moving—through at one mile per hour."

Again Yakov gave the word, and the copter jerked itself upward, the rotors clawing the sky. "We're due in Valdez by four," he said. "Wouldn't want to be late for chow."

The rest of the trip was uneventful, and again the individual team members fell into silence, their minds troubled. Some recalled the Fort Greely stopover early Christmas morning—there they had heard eyewitness accounts of the slaughter. Seven men dead, including the hapless guard; one severely wounded.

Someone would pay. In spades.

But when it came to the bottom line, it was the

same as in Seattle. No loose ends. Nothing left behind. Nobody at the Army base had gotten a fix on any of the Grey Dog terrorists.

The witnesses said a heavy helicopter had set down, a highly trained kill force, numbers unknown, had charged out and made mincemeat of the dazed personnel. The terrorists had known which building housed the weapons cache; they had known what they wanted and had seized it with dispatch, even remembering parts kits in their haste.

One thing was certain, the Irish renegades were armed to the teeth. If Hal Brognola's body count was on the money, each man had an M-16 for every other day of the week.

Ransome pointed out landmarks as they moved south: the pipeline bridge at the Yukon River and its accompanying pumping station—the first permanent crossing of the river in Alaskan history. The rotors blasted through the foothills near Livengood. Then a refueling stop at Fairbanks. Mount McKinley, highest point in North America, loomed on their left. Southward to the Tanana River, where a 1200-foot span of pipe shifted the oil south. Tanana, site of Fort Greely, made a special impression. Now the 650-foot bridge across the Tazlina stood below them.

By then things had begun to blur. The harsh scenery added up to but one thing—an almost inhuman, insurmountable challenge for Phoenix Force.

It was 1550 hours when the pilot broke into the

team's deepening funk. "Valdez coming up, gentlemen," he announced. "We'll be setting down in five minutes."

"Kindly check for all personal belongings," McCarter quipped. "Especially your bloody brats. Please take all small children by the hand...."

5

Two geodesic domes, dimly glowing, poked their heads above the raging, twenty-foot-high sheets of blowing snow. A bank of radar shields flanked the USAF top-secret installation, while inside the electronic palisade, radio-telescopic dish antennas scanned the skies around the clock. The adjoining buildings housing the Satellite Control Facility—two, long, arctic-reinforced, Quonset-type barracks—issued the faintest speck of light from random windows and door tunnels, snowdrifts piled almost to the eaves.

The relentless storm obliterated even the puny traces of human habitation upon the endless, barren ice plain that was the North Slope.

But inside the billeting area, usually occupied by a fifteen-man USAF complement, all was calm. The blizzard's howl was muted by the constant hum of the fans and by the mutter and laughter—even at 2300 hours—of the Grey Dog invaders.

In one room, originally intended for two Air Force technicians, five Irish hardmen were crowded around a table playing poker. The two bunks in the room had been jammed together to make room for three bedrolls on the floor. It was the same in all the rooms opening on the corridor, except in the room occupied by the topcock, Sean Toolan.

Other Grey Dog personnel maintained a haphazard patrol of the storage, mess and power-generating areas of the second building. In the main dome, a skeleton crew of terrified, dog-tired controllers spelled one another in the monitoring of the instrumentation contained therein. They kept open communication lines between AFSAT-COM in Denver, between backup installations at Eileson and Shemya Air Force bases in Alaska, and between advance-warning stations at Cambridge Bay, Canada and Thule, Greenland.

All part of an interconnected early-warning link, none of the sister installations could be allowed to suspect that they were under siege. To stress the point, the terrorists aimed pistols at each GI's head during every minute, every hour of the crewman's watch.

The illusion of normalcy must be preserved at all cost, Toolan had roared, vowing to skin alive any of his forty-four soldiers who might allow their captives to leak an alert to the outside world during routine transmissions. Six days remained before a relief crew would be flown in from Eileson AFB; the terrorists must be long gone before then.

The computer consoles winked and clicked, the digital counters flickered nonstop. The huge interior dishes and radio beacons made their precise, clock-driven rounds. Computerized printouts flashed in from matching consoles at all privileged stations. And from the terrorist-conquered site, located on the Colville River, halfway between Umiat and the Beaufort Sea, roughly a hundred sixty miles west of Prudhoe, lulling word went out: everything was copacetic.

The attack on QSS 0022 had been swift and deadly, the double copter landing obscured by eternal night and by ceaseless wind-howl. The attack had been abetted by the smug, insular over-confidence of the military men within. Before the nerve-center personnel could even think to zap Mayday into the Arctic ozone, they had found the icy muzzles of the M-16s snugly pressed to their temples.

Lieutenant Grant Pollard, his nose caved in, three fingers on his right hand shattered by a rifle butt, had quickly babbled all security codes and procedures to Toolan and Cafferty, and had instructed his com-center technicians to cooperate to the fullest with the terrorists.

The facility commander had never been seen again.

So, in the dead of the Alaskan hibernation. . . .

Business as usual.

At that moment, in the lieutenant's quarters, now commandeered by Sean Toolan, a scene of domesticity was unfolding.

Coletta Devane, clad in a navy blue robe formerly owned by Pollard, emerged from the bathroom, freshly showered, applying finishing touches to her fiery tresses with a brush. "Some place, huh, love?'' she addressed Toolan. ''A regular Taj Mahal. These Yanks really go first class, don't they?''

Toolan, sprawled in a chair in one corner of the room, looked up from the glass of Scotch he was regarding. ''Nice enough, I guess,'' he muttered. ''Don't go gettin' used to it now. It's a nasty bit o' work we have before us.''

She put down the brush, shook out her hair. She lifted the half-empty bottle and frowned. ''Work like this is it, man?''

''Don't start again, woman,'' he snapped. ''A man's entitled to a dram now and then. It's been a raw day.''

''All your days are raw, Sean. Keep it up, and Bryan will be finishing this mission, mark my word.''

''Is that all you know, Col? If I needed nagging I'd have remained home with me mother.''

Devane jutted one hip provocatively at him, the robe falling partially open to reveal smooth slender legs. ''Just as well, I suppose,'' she sneered. ''Sure an' bejasus she'd ask no odds of you.''

''A real broken record you are, Col,'' he blustered, no real steam behind the words. He averted his eyes. ''Is sex all you ever think of? I thought we took care of that just last night.''

''Use it or lose it,'' she smirked. ''That's what I always say, darlin'.''

When he did not answer but continued to sullenly suck back the liquor, she said, ''Maybe I should peddle my fish elsewhere, duck? There's men down the hall who wouldn't have to be asked twice. Always had a curiosity in me t'see how many men I could take on in one night. It's a common female fantasy.''

''Well,'' he gritted, ''go do it then. If that's what you want. I swear, I don't know what to make of you. Go, then.''

Her eyes softened, a winsome yearning reflected there. ''But don't you see, Sean?'' She sighed. ''That's *not* what I want. What I want is you. What's gone wrong? You used to be so eager. You couldn't get enough of me. What happened?'' She sank onto his lap, wound her arms around his head, dragged his face to her breasts. She opened the robe and guided his fingers to the swollen nipples.

''Dammit, Coletta,'' he protested, ''can't you see I ain't in the mood?''

Her eyes glittered. ''Maybe I could get you in the mood, lover,'' she sighed. She dislodged herself and slid between his thighs. She began opening his clothes.

''Jesus, Mary and Joseph,'' he muttered, feebly forestalling her bold fingers. ''Don't be doing that. It's a blot in God's eyes. *Coletta!*'' He jerked, stiffened as he felt her hot lancing tongue. Then, a moment later, the suffocating wet heat of her mouth.

''Coletta...'' he groaned. ''You bitch. You *sweet* bitch.''

Outdoors the wind had picked up, whipping viciously at the exposed corners of the buildings.

The temperature stood at thirty below, the wind-chill factor at seventy-five below. It was, in truth, hell's deep freeze.

In one sheltered angle where the buildings butted, lay a grisly scene—nine airmen, bodies flung heedlessly, like so much cordwood, all frozen in a grotesque tangle. Some lay flat, eyes distended, wide with horror. Others were contorted, limbs askew, mouths open wide, where they had pleaded to the last against the killer's single bullet to the brain.

Minute by minute the blizzard layered the bodies with snow. An hour later all were covered, placed in frozen storage until spring would find them again.

6

"Good morning, ladies and gentlemen," Jack Grimaldi said, his dark eyes flashing. "This is your tour director speaking. Today we'll be taking an exciting excursion to Alaska's fascinating North Slope, where we'll spend hours exploring the Trans-Alaska Pipeline. Now if you'll look out the window on your left...."

"Turn if off," Rafael Encizo protested, smiling despite himself. "Travelogues we don't need."

Dispatched directly from a successful mission in Japan, Grimaldi, Stony Man's free-lance flying ace, had joined Phoenix Force in Valdez late the previous night.

Now manning the controls of an Army issue Bell Long Ranger, Grimaldi, his brown, curly hair in disarray, his bulky frame at ease in the helicopter's flight seat, was carefully checking the pipeline's northernmost meanderings. Hovering at thirty feet, moving at snail's pace, they searched for signs of unauthorized activity below.

And though each member of Phoenix Force seethed inwardly at the apparent futility of the search, each knew it was their only course of action.

There had been no break in the info blackout. No more Grey Dog raids, no sign of movement on any front. It was as if the Arctic had swallowed them up.

So. Run the pipeline. Foot by foot, mile by mile.

Phoenix was not alone on search-and-destroy. The U.S. Army was laboriously gearing up for a pipeline patrol of its own. At this moment, farther south between the Yukon and Valdez, military copters were up, running the same drills as Katz and his team. And, from Fort Richardson at Anchorage, and Fort Wainwright at Fairbanks, Sikorsky S-65s were being loaded with troops. Simultaneously Sikorsky CH-54Bs were sky-hooking to M113 APC's—armored personnel carriers. Other M113s were being shipped to the closest railheads; they would proceed overland from there.

The sky cranes would be lowering the first of the APCs at Prudhoe to provide perimeter defense later in the afternoon.

The INLA would find a formidable welcoming committee waiting should they be foolhardy enough to launch a frontal attack on the critical installation.

To Colonel Yakov Katzenelenbogen, seated next to Grimaldi—the cocksure pilot never tolerated a copilot—it was poor tactics. Deterrent force was no way to fight a war.

And while he fumed, Katz pondered their plan. Locate the INLA hideout. Hit them hard, demolish them to the last man, before that first slab of C-3 could even be placed.

Which brought them back to square one.

Grimaldi and the Bell 206L. The gray snake belly-winding itself across the bleak landscape.

Repeatedly Katz put the Bausch & Lomb 10x50 binoculars to his eyes and surveyed the contrast-less terrain unfolding bleak, unvarying beneath the chopper. Frustration mounted.

"Please remember, folks," Grimaldi said, try-ing to cut the tension, "while it doesn't look like much, Exxon, Arco, British Petroleum and all the rest have spared no expense in bringing this ma-jestic wonder to you. Two years in the building, it cost over eight *billion* dollars before it was com-pleted in 1977. The line pumps two million barrels of crude into Valdez every day of the year. Not only that, dear travelers, but...."

"Knock it off, will you," Encizo objected.

"A cast of thousands...." Grimaldi persisted.

"Enough." It was Yakov who cut Grimaldi off this time. "We are quite familiar with that PR."

"Bears repeating." Grimaldi grinned, in no way squelched. "It's the engineering feat of the cen-tury."

"So, I'm impressed," the Phoenix headman snapped. "Now may we go on to other things?"

Today, at 1500 hours, they were again working toward the foothills of the Brooks range, all con-vinced that if Grey Dog had established a base camp, the craggy, forested terrain would be the most logical place for it. As the endless snow

prairie gradually gave way to the first outcroppings of rock—jet black against the luminous
whiteness—the team stirred and searched the
gloom more intently.

The pipeline eased down off its stilts, dug slowly
into an underground bedding, duplicating the con-
tours of moraine scree and talus, high-legging it
again when the bottom dropped out too precipi-
tously.

The day was more murky than before, cloud
cover concealing the stars—a storm definitely
brewing.

Ohara studied the terrain beneath the slow-
moving chopper, his eyes on super fine-tune.
Abruptly, glimpsing a shadowy muddling in the
snow near one stretch of pipe, a trail streaking to
the left, his pulse quickened. He adjusted, straining harder to see.

They were near Toolik—pumping station three,
according to their charts—a likely spot for sabotage. Then suddenly, a movement off to the left.
Keio jerked and sucked in a quick breath. "Down
there." He pointed. "Something moved."

Instantly everyone's nose was pressed to the
glass. Desperate eyes followed Ohara's finger to
an expanse of meadow, over which the TAP again
rode its steel trestles.

"Swing her around, Jack," Katz ordered.
"Let's have a second look."

This time the Bell Long Ranger came in lower
and executed an agonizingly slow pass over the
area. "There," Encizo said excitedly, "I see it.

Just past that rock pile to the right. All kinds of tracks there. But there's nobody around."

"Maybe some caribou yarding," Manning offered. "Wildlife of some sort. A grizzly with insomnia. . . ."

"Wildlife, all right," McCarter snorted. "Goddamned micks is what it is. They got a ripe smell all their own." Instantly he lifted his AK-47. "How about it, Yakov? We go down?"

Katz turned to Grimaldi. "Take us down, Jack. Off to the left there. Give us some distance so we're out of range if they are down there."

Immediately there was flurry of activity in the crowded cabin, everyone checking his weapons, strapping on ammo belts, securing snaps and zippers on their Arctic jump suits. Special fur-lined leather gloves were donned. Their parkas were snugged tight, the cowl almost hiding their faces. Wool face masks were pulled down.

"How'n hell are we gonna fight in all this?" Rafael said. "I feel like a walking mountain."

"Don't knock it," McCarter replied. "Your blood'll turn to ice without that stuff on."

"Remember your orientation," Yakov reminded everyone as the helicopter settled into the snow, and the team crowded the door. "Move slowly, with deliberation. Keep your hood up. No quick breaths. You'll freeze your lungs. Keep your gloves on at all times, no matter what. Otherwise," he saluted briefly with his steel claw, "you'll have fingers like mine."

And then, as the door was forced open, ice falling like brittle glass along the seams, Yakov said, "Spread out as we approach the line. We play it by ear after that." He called back into the cabin, "Keep your radio open, Jack. In case we need some help."

Moments later the five men were down, weapons ready, scuttling away from the rotor backwash as fast as they dared. The wind tore at their eyes and fought for entry at every careless opening in their gear. It was fifteen below, but the windchill drove the temperature to fifty below within seconds, hammering home the meaning of the term, flash freezing.

All weapons had been treated with CLP, an application of submicron Teflon particles suspended in a special solvent. The guns were free of all traces of oil, which would freeze.

Grateful for the long fur about their faces, they began slogging slowly through the knee-high snow, eyes darting, alert for any telltale movement ahead.

The pipeline, dimly outlined against the clouding snow, lay a quarter mile away. Pausing often, searching the brush, the pine and tamarack stands, they advanced, foot by cautious foot.

At the base of the line, the forty-eight-inch pipe looming overhead, they studied the tracks around one set of VSMs and saw caked snow on a cross trestle, a clear indication someone had climbed up.

"What did I tell you?" McCarter chortled, examining the tracks, following them to the left, where they trailed up a slight rise and disappeared over a second hill. "Paddies, sure's hell. Six or eight of 'em from the looks of it."

He was champing at the bit to be off in pursuit. "Just left, I'll bet. Heard our chopper and broomed off." His eyes were expectant. "We go after 'em, eh, Katz?"

Katz silenced him with a brusque wave. "What do you see, Gary?" he asked Manning, who had climbed up the steel piling and was carefully examining the pipe.

"Nothing here. No sign of any explosive device at all. McCarter's right; we must have scared them off."

Katz then got on the Johnson 577 and directed Grimaldi to fly a quick recon. They were splitting up, he told Grimaldi, heading into the high country. The ace pilot complied and was racketing over their heads within a minute.

"Got a fix on you guys," his voice crackled. "I'm heading out."

"Keep some distance," Katz cautioned. "Even the Cong brought down helicopters with rifles."

"Got you, chief. On course." The Bell Long Ranger swung sharply on its rotors, quickly disappeared over the treetops.

"McCarter—" Yakov pointed direction "—you and Keio take the right flank. The rest of us will shake out the left. Spread out. No shooting unless it's absolutely necessary. Got your two-way, Keio?"

"Check."

"And don't get too far afield. This storm is definitely picking up. I don't want anybody lost in this mess."

The team split up and headed out.

"They must have a chopper stashed back there somewhere," Encizo said as they slogged deeper into the brush, stopping often to watch and listen for any movement ahead. By now their face masks were rimmed with ice, their eyelids heavily frosted.

"More than likely," Yakov replied. Then, shortly, there was excitement in his voice. "Then again, they could have come overland. Perhaps from that base camp we've been breaking our ass to find. Maybe we've stumbled onto something at last."

Hearts revved up, fresh hope was born. Trigger fingers suddenly developed a bad itch. And yet there were doubts; such a turn would be altogether unexpected.

Things seldom came easy for Phoenix Force.

Yakov's radio came to life. "Got something here," Grimaldi's voice crackled. "Movement on the left side of the pipe. Heading east in quite a scamper. I figure five hundred yards ahead of your present position. Bring it on up."

"Any sign of a copter?" Yakov questioned.

"Negative. But that doesn't mean it isn't there. Our storm is here. Visibility's near zero. Barely make out the troops. We got ten minutes at best before we do a Dunkirk."

"Not yet," Yakov said firmly. "Stand by. We'll take our chances."

"Got a fix here," Keio's voice came on the second the pilot broke transmission. "A couple of stragglers. We're moving into your zone."

"Get a live one if you can," Yakov said. "We need information in the worst way."

"Okay," Keio came back. "Repeat. Moving into your zone."

They pushed forward with as much vigor as they dared, Rafael and Manning drifting even farther left for an extreme flank and possible cutoff. Their boots crashed through the undergrowth and the caked snow. One moment they hurried across a solid surface, the next they dropped through to their waists in snow. Manning pinched his parka shut over his mouth to allow deeper breathing. The wind speed was twenty-five miles per hour.

The clatter of the Bell's rotors became louder. Grimaldi, the original crazy man, was flying over the fleeing Grey Dogs, all but begging for a gut shot.

They heard the distant pop-pop-pop of rifle fire to their right.

The three men cursed in frustration, dug their feet furiously into the slippery slope, gasping in their eagerness to get on the line before it was all over. The weather was not cooperating with their efforts. Falling, blowing snow obscured trees ten feet away.

The gunfire was closer. As Yakov, Rafael and Manning came over a thirty-foot incline, they could barely make out the battle arena. The pipeline glowed eerily through the screen of snow.

Sporadic muzzle-flashes—merest fire-pricks in the darkness—ignited to their right. Return sparks could not be seen; the Grey Dog force was apparently nailed down in a protective, stone-shouldered shelter.

"Must be Keio and McCarter," Rafael said, indicating the activity closest to the pipeline.

Fifty yards ahead, on a higher bank, secondary gunfire erupted, the bark throaty, hollow, the chatter on the slow side.

"Sounds like a Sten to me," Manning muttered, at once shifting, aiming his CAR-15 at the hardman's lair, forty feet above the main assault zone.

He cursed softly as the trigger depressed and nothing happened. Manual action then. Finally, with a studied slam of the magazine section against a tree, the frozen part came unstuck. Anger filled him as he accepted blame for the half-assed winterizing of his weapon. He knew his gaffe was inexcusable. Any other time the miscue could have meant instant death.

He opened up on the terrorist's nest, sending a half-dozen rounds, the CAR's muzzle-flash spitting a full four inches, illuminating the hard planes of his face. Gary then saw Yakov moving out, darting and dropping in short bursts down the incline.

"Coming in, Keio," Yakov blurted into the Johnson portable, "at ten o'clock. Rafael and Gary are trying to sweep. How many you got?"

"Three, I think. Hey, they're on the move.

Out." The radio went dead. Red-hot slugs punched into the terrorists' shelter. Then there was a smear in the dusk, the Phoenix duo sliding right to throw off their quarry and the hillside sniper in the bargain.

Yakov, advancing in a crabbed crouch on the enemy's blind side, added pin-down rounds of his own.

From the corner of his eye Yakov saw Manning and Encizo, smudged wraiths in the deepening storm, laboriously working their way up the bluff.

"Spot 'em?" McCarter gasped, the extended exertion getting to him. "We must've winged one of those bastards at least." He spit. "Rather be shooting to kill, if you ask me."

"No," Keio murmured, the Arctic cold making inroads on his remarkable endurance as well. "They're holed up again. Did you bring a grenade? That'll flush them out."

"It just so happens...." McCarter chuckled. He grunted against the binding winter gear and plucked an M-26 from his cartridge belt. Another grunt, a click as the pin came out. The tinny clatter of the ejecting handle. Then the grenade was swooshing through the air, homing on the Grey Dog position.

The afternoon was torn apart by a flat, metallic concussion. Raising their heads, they saw a glittering afterglow, a rainbow of death captured in the scattering snowflakes. They heard a single agonized scream, a fresh rattle of submachine-gun fire.

"Pay dirt," McCarter yipped. "Blood on the snow."

Yakov, well out of range, lurched up, using the diversion to move still closer to the enemy. He keyed the radio. "I'm moving in," he informed Ohara. "Give me high fire."

For an answer the two men opened up with an M-16 and an AK-47, deliberately aiming above the terrorists' heads. Instantly they rolled away to avoid incoming rounds.

In that moment Katz darted forward another twenty-five feet and got a clear fix on the crew. There were three of them, one writhing in the snow, the others hunkered down in a stony cul-de-sac. He belly-crawled closer, his white suit and the storm granting almost total camouflage. He lay still, prepared to perform battlefield lobotomy.

It was then that the overhead scout saw the Phoenix Force member. The Sten Mark 6 cut loose, and Yakov felt the smashing impact in the ground, the slugs tearing up solid rock to his right, chips spattering his face. Acting on sheer reflex he rolled left as four more rounds blazed in, pounding the spot he had just occupied.

The remaining hardmen, seeing the commotion, spun, prepared to finish Katz off. They relished the prospect.

They waited one second too long. McCarter and Keio charged forward with matching instinct. Orders forgotten, murder in their hearts, they started a savage fire on the surviving terrorists, sending a combined forty rounds into their lair, chopping them into stewing meat. Sheets of blood spread out around their bodies, forming stark, black stains in the snow.

Up on the hill the panicky scout rose to kneeling position, crazy to exact gory retribution of his own. He fired three wild shots, then discovered his weapon was empty.

Cursing, he dropped back and groped for a fresh magazine with cold-deadened hands. He was just slapping it into his Sten when he realized he was not alone.

Two men, their assault rifles poised in unmistakable menace, towered over him. "Hold it right there, mister," Encizo barked, hard put to keep excitement from his voice. A live one Yakov had said. This was just what the doctor ordered. "Put the piece down. *Drop it, I said.*"

But the terrorist was no fool; he knew exactly what lay in store for him should he be taken alive. With a swift, sideways lunge the scout deliberately propelled himself over the edge of the outcropping on which he had chosen to make his stand.

Two rifles blasted in tandem bass, aiming low. The scout rolled headlong down the hill, his maimed legs unable to provide any braking traction. Twenty feet down he struck his head on a rock, the impact snapping his neck like a brittle twig.

He was dead long before his fur-swathed body came to rest at the bottom of the hill.

There was no time for pursuit of the remaining members of the terrorist force. Even through the increasing howl of the wind, the snow descending in buckets, they detected the distant thunder of a helicopter as it gained altitude about five hundred yards to the south. The rotors clacked more rapidly, and the sound faded, the craft fleeing deeper into the Brooks mountain range.

Instantly Katzenelenbogen was on the Johnson. "Grimaldi," he bawled, "do you see that chopper? Any chance of us catching it? If you could drop down here fast, pick us up...."

"No way, Colonel," the pilot rasped. "In the first place I can't see the other bird. In the second, I'm having trouble holding this one on track. Another five minutes and I can't guarantee taking us out of this. I'm coming down. We go. Fast."

The men of Phoenix Force were decidedly humbled by this firsthand demonstration of the awesome power of nature on the rampage. As they went through the clothing and rucksacks of the dead hardmen, searching for clues—identity, location of the hideout, actual mission—they wondered which was the worst enemy. The Alaskan winter or Grey Dog?

"They're not holding any demolition gear," Manning yelled over the wail of the blizzard. "Maybe it was just a scouting mission. Or else the hard stuff went on ahead with the forward party; these heroes were just covering ass."

Encizo picked up one of the M-16s, casually snapped congealed gore off it with his glove before slinging the gun over his shoulder. "I'll bet any money that these came from Greely."

Grimaldi brought the Bell Long Ranger down cautiously, homing on the MK-13 flare Manning had wisely packed. The five men clambered aboard, each appalled by the intense effort the simple act took, their fingers, arms and legs turned to wood by the relentless, strength-sapping cold. Before the door could be closed, two inches of snow had blown into the cabin.

McCarter stared dully into space as the chopper jerked up. "Bloody hell..." he intoned in a despairing monotone, demoralized by the setback.

His nose was running; drops of water from his thawing eyebrows cascaded down in a steady drip.

His dejection was contagious. Every man in the cabin knew he had been in a fight with hell. White hell.

7

"And just where in hell have the filthy, rotten bastards got to?" Yakov Katzenelenbogen gritted, his usually imperturbable demeanor marred by rage, his scowl cowing even McCarter.

"Easy does it, guv," McCarter ventured softly. "The weather hasn't been exactly cooperating, you know."

"Weather be damned. We're just shifting blame if we fall back on that. We were out the better part of yesterday...once that blasted storm blew out. We'll be out all day today. We've patrolled our stretch on the TAP six times. And what have we accomplished? Absolutely nothing."

Two days had passed since Phoenix's clash with the storm, and this morning, at 0900 hours, the team was again airborne, Grimaldi humming tunelessly at the controls, a U.S. Army Sikorsky S-45 plugging along in their wake. There was a slight pewter cast to the sky; stars twinkled merrily. On the horizon the northern lights were putting on a spectacular show, the layered, floating waves of color blinding. Good weather for a ground patrol.

"The Army's uncovered nothing either. And

when will they show themselves? Certainly they didn't come here for the skiing." He lapsed into Yiddish. Which he invariably did when he wanted to purge his frustration.

Yesterday Phoenix had returned to the Toolik pumping-station area. They had donned snow-shoes and had gone overland in all directions in hope of stumbling on fresh spoor. But there was nothing. The blizzard had covered all trace of the Grey Dog dead, all footpaths as well.

Alternating between air and foot patrol, they had scoured every foot of the pipeline in the area for evidence of new terrorist movement. They had dropped down on every dismantled work camp in their quadrant and had reassured themselves that no secret underground burrows had been dug.

And beyond that—the U.S. Army coming up equally empty—what was there? They had consulted with long-time TAP personnel, eliminating all other possibles. The barge hulks in the Beau-fort Sea, trapped since 1974? The offshore drilling platforms?

Quick reconnaissance had established that these were vermin free. The barges were deserted, haunted only by howling winds. As for the drill hands? Dirty, raunchy, irreverent, resentful, eager to get back to their $32.80 an hour. Fleas perhaps, but no Grey Dogs.

"What kind of weather report have we got to-day?" Rafael Encizo asked, staring glumly from the window at the desolate scenery below. The snow reflected a leaden luster, clouds of snow blowing fifty feet high in places, the terrain lined with endless dunes, a ribbing resembling waves, an eternal tide pool of ice and snow.

"Another storm due later," Grimaldi replied, "but nothing serious. We should be back to base before it hits."

"And another day wasted," Katz fumed. "When will those swine make their move?"

"If it's any consolation," Manning interjected, "the weather's keeping the Irish on a short leash also. They're getting hurt more than we are by these delays. We can afford to outwait them."

"Do you suppose," Keio Ohara suggested, "that we might be limiting our search too much? Maybe their base is a hundred, perhaps two hundred miles away."

"Could be that some alien force just beams them down here during certain hours of the day," McCarter jeered.

"But where?" Yakov persisted, considering Keio's idea. "It would be almost impossible for them to set up that far away. They don't have the network for that."

"Don't they?" Keio's expression was arch. "Remember, some time back, how that Jeddah outfit infiltrated the military. Who's to say it isn't the same story here?"

"It's possible," Manning agreed. "There could be someone masterminding the whole thing right in the midst of that Prudhoe hornets' nest. Outsmarting us at every turn."

"But why?" Yakov came back, his mind distracted. "What does the inside agent hope to gain?"

"Why does anyone sell out?" Keio said. "Money. I mean big dollars. There's always some malcontent in the woodwork, someone nursing an imagined grudge. If the INLA, thanks to some wealthy sheikh, could pass along a half million, tax free...."

"That's a bit farfetched." Yakov rejected the theory. "No," he sighed. "I think it's a simple hit-and-run with no long-range planning involved. That's why I say they're in the immediate area." But there was not that much conviction in his words; it was obvious that certain wheels were grudgingly beginning to turn inside his brain.

But for now they all turned to the work at hand.

Today Phoenix would venture farther afield in the Brooks range foothills. Where previously the width of their search had been limited by the Arctic inroads on human endurance, this morning they would spread across fifty miles of the landscape paralleling the pipeline's right flank. Mounted on snowmobiles, they would move deeper into the foothills. Returning in the afternoon, they would do the same for the TAP's left flank.

Last night, in crash indoctrination, they had driven for hours into the Prudhoe countryside. An expert snowmobiler had put them through rigorous paces, explaining all emergency procedures.

And now, arriving at a lowland site twenty miles north of Toolik, Grimaldi began losing altitude.

The Sikorsky also dropped. Again there was a flurry of activity inside the Bell. Weapons were checked, ammo stashed, special equipment packed into rucksacks. Emergency rations were divided among the team members. And finally, the chore of shagging into cold-weather gear, into boot-packs, into gloves. Again they became walking mountains of down, fur and wool.

As they slung their rifles over their shoulders, Encizo noticed a bulky package partially hidden behind their makeshift arsenal. He pulled away a blanket to reveal an abbreviated bazooka-type weapon. "Who brought this monstrosity aboard?" he asked. "What in hell is it?"

Manning answered, "It's something I picked up at Fort Greely when we were loading up. It's a Dragon M-47 antitank weapon."

"Tank weapon?" Keio jumped in. "You're going to take on our own troops now? Grey Dog hasn't lifted any tanks. Not that I've heard of anyway."

Manning was defensive. "It was just an afterthought," he said. "I figured we might be running up against a hideout of sorts, a mountain dig-in or some such. And since we don't have artillery...no cannon on the chopper.... Who can tell? It might come in handy."

The blanket was dropped. Quizzical looks were sent Manning's way as they prepared for landfall.

As Phoenix emerged from the Bell, boots creaking on the subzero hardpan of snow and ice, the hovering Sikorsky's deck was slowly coming down. Five Finncats—the Cadillac of snowmobiles—were lined up on the platform. Made by VPLO Industries in Finland, the Finncat was the most dependable, most economical and most responsive snowmobile in existence.

As they approached the Sikorsky, waiting for the platform to touch down, McCarter was already bitching. "My poor aching ass. The drubbing that thing gave me last night."

"Which accounts for your muddled mental state this morning, I suppose?" Rafael smiled.

"How's that, mate? Come again?"

"Seeing as your brains are located in your ass, no wonder everything's cloudy for you today."

"Kindly piss up a rope," McCarter replied with a grin.

Then they were kicking the Finncats to life, carefully edging them off the cargo deck, nursing the engines to full, throaty roar. Gas supplies were checked, and extra equipment was stored forward in customized storage compartments.

As Gary Manning placed an extra long, scabbarded knife into his bin, Keio asked, "What the hell is that, another brainstorm? Are you setting out to cut sugarcane or something?"

Manning's smile was evasive. "My Alaskan survival kit," he said simply, letting it drop.

Ten minutes later Phoenix Force was ready for jump off. From the cockpits of the two helicopters, the pilots—Grimaldi in one, two Army men in the other—watched, glad they were to remain behind. Engines killed, an interior generator-heater running at low throttle, they would await the team's return, late that afternoon. Radio contact would remain constant, with each member carrying a unit.

There was a final briefing on position and Mayday procedures by Katz. Then the snowmobile convoy was off in a boil of bluish gray smoke.

The lightweight, fiberglass Finncats had no skis. Instead they were fully tracked from front to back, steering on the same principle as a tank: lock the left track to go left, the right to go right. They had a top speed of forty miles per hour and could cross any type of terrain—tundra, sand, underbrush, steep incline—where the conventional snowmobile was meant for snow alone. And low-incline snow at that.

Each man had been instructed to maintain a five-mile distance, establish frequent radio contact, keep to an average speed of twenty miles per hour, with turnback toward the pipeline slated for noon. During this mission, the Finncat's single headlight would be operational.

It was 1000 hours when Yakov, taking the five-mile track, received word from Encizo to head out. The inner track was his deliberate choice; still holding to his conviction that Grey Dog was skulking nearby.

At the outset the going was relatively easy, and by watching his compass, Katz was able to hold a straight course. But as he proceeded, he found the going got rougher with each additional mile. Time and time again he was forced to backtrack, make a sidelong pass at particularly rugged hogbacks. His speed was constantly cut.

The Finncat was a sweet piece of machinery, with excellent stability and amazing traction. Its center of gravity superb, it clung to twenty-five-degree slopes effortlessly, and all fears of overturning were quickly dismissed.

The temperature stood at twenty below, but the forward thrust of the snowmobile dropped that to sixty below. The high fairing granted enough protection so that the compactly built Israeli only suffered minor agony. His one hand, shoulders and feet began getting cold first, and he was forced to flex his fingers, twist his torso, stamp his feet intermittently. There was, however, no danger of frostbite. The wintersuit saw to that.

Yakov's eyes darted nonstop from side to side as he searched the underbrush, probed swales and valleys below him and studied the higher elevations. There was a hypnotic monotony to the lurching, swerving ride, and there were times when the darkness contributed a further lulling effect.

Often he braked and throttled the engine back to a soft purr. He listened for sounds, watched for movement. Repeatedly, when he saw outcroppings of rock resembling a camouflaged rooftop or a group of hastily constructed cabins, he veered off course and swept down for a closer look.

But it was always just an optical illusion, and nothing more.

He pressed on.

The snarling drone of the snow-machine's engine enhanced the surrealistic mood. Alert, Katz knew full well that danger might be lurking just ahead.

His was not a foolhardy, arrogant overconfidence, however. It came under the name of experience.

Some might call it déjà vu. The case-hardened warrior had been here before. Four decades of living on the brink of death were guarantee that he was more than equal to any challenge that might crop up. To the fifty-five-year-old ex-Mossad agent in the Israeli army, survival was a mere matter of knowing when to duck, when to charge forward.

He had survived the *Boche*—Nazi bastards—in Paris, when as a boy, he had run courier for the underground. He had survived Hanoi when Ho Chi Minh had been laying groundwork for Vietnam. He had survived the founding of the Israeli nation. He had fought as a young man with Ben-Gurion against the Arab and English jackals—which were the more treacherous he could never decide.

He had survived the Six Day War in 1967—although not totally, for he had left part of his right arm on that bloody killing ground.

And he had suffered an even more grievous loss—a son, Torem, had been killed in yet another sector of that same battle.

As if that was not tragedy enough, in 1974 Katz had lost his wife, Cynthia, in a late-night automobile accident. According to the police, she had gone to sleep at the wheel. But Yakov knew better; he knew the "accident" was terrorist conceived. One day soon, he thought, he would settle scores on that one.

Katz shifted his five-nine, 185-pound frame on the snowmobile seat and tried to shake off the morbid memories. *What good is it to dredge up that stuff,* he asked himself.

He was, beneath it all, a warm, kind, jovial and peace-loving man. He fought with Phoenix Force only to preserve peace—he felt it was something worth dying for.

He recalled his last interlude with Jerusha and how she had begged him to retire. She would divorce her husband, marry Yakov; she would move heaven and earth to make him happy, to become a worthy successor to Cynthia.

He had been tempted. Jerusha was a magnificent woman; he loved her dearly. But in the end, he had not hesitated for a moment when Colonel John Phoenix had summoned him for this latest mission.

Regrettably Jerusha would continue to occupy second place in his life. There are men who talk of peace. There are others who do something about it.

And yes, he agreed in near lament, he might be getting past his prime, a bit heavy in the middle, his hair thinning. But he was still a man.

He was still a survivor.

And heaven help the miserable bastard who might try to alter that status.

The grim-faced man cursed in Yiddish again, jammed out his right foot to prevent a tip-over, an unseen log presenting a chance for disaster. *Alter kocker,* he castigated. *You old fool. Keep your mind on what you're doing.*

On the far end of the search quadrant, Encizo was encountering smooth sailing; he would be in port well ahead of the others.

Like Katz, he was finding no sign of enemy activity. "Hey, McCarter," he called into his walkie-talkie to the man patrolling his left, "enjoying the ride? Ain't you glad we came to Alaska instead of Hawaii? I'm spotting nothing here. Rocks and snow. *Nada más.*"

McCarter keyed his radio, replied snidely, "Ten-four, Rafael. I got me a couple of cow seals here. Both in heat. They been askin' about you. Other than that, nothing much to report."

"I'll pass on the seals," Encizo shot back.

McCarter had tipped over once and had struggled furiously to right his Finncat. Stymied by a series of cross-ridges, he knew he was lagging. Now he roared his engine, aimed into a meadow at full clip.

On his left, Manning had drawn his Finncat to full stop and had killed the engine. Off to one side, caught in the glare of his headlight, was a blinking, scowling golden grizzly. Perched on the side of a hill, a shadowy area behind indicated his den; he would easily weigh nine hundred pounds, and though scruffy from hibernation, he was a fantastic specimen.

Manning watched the bear for a few minutes more. But as the minor mountain became restless and made a tentative move toward him, Manning sparked the snowmobile to life and eased forward. At least, he thought, as he threw up blinding clouds of snow, he had something to show for his ride.

Keio Ohara was similarly disgusted. Two-thirds of the allotted territory covered, and he had yet to see anything that even remotely resembled trouble. And they had another afternoon of this before them?

At first he had been grateful for the solitude; there had been moments for meditation, and he had achieved an inner detachment of sorts. It had provided a resurgence of soul and had let him escape the penetrating cold.

But through the minor nirvana, there remained a nagging presentiment of doom; he was fielding psychic emanations he could not begin to identify. Something was definitely wrong.

Had he lifted his eyes, forgotten his scouting chores for a moment, he might have noticed that the sky was rapidly clouding over, the array of stars winking out overhead. He might have noticed an abrupt shifting of the wind.

But no, dedicated soldier that he was, he concentrated on the terrain unwinding below him. Neither Keio nor any of the others noticed the distinct weather change until it was too late.

EVEN AS THE TEAM ATE tasteless Army rations from individual insulated carriers—all gathered around a roaring fire Manning had ignited with an extra flare—they still failed to recognize encroaching jeopardy. The fire, the food, the windbreak, provided by the pipeline VSRs, helped isolate them from reality.

But shortly, as the sand-hard snow became driving arrows, and wind gusts all but ripped their parkas away, pummeled their bodies with haymaker impact, they took notice.

"Hey," Keio exclaimed, nearly flattened by a particularly severe blast. "And we're going to ride against that?"

Katz's face grave, he ducked behind a Finncat, signaled Grimaldi, fifty miles to the north. "Where the hell does your weatherman get his forecasts?" he shouted. "From a fortune cookie? This is a squall? We've got at least a forty-mile wind here. I think we'd best call it a day. We'll ditch the Finncats, recover them later. Come pick us up, Jack."

The signal was weak, Grimaldi's voice fading in and out, at times disappearing completely. "Negative, guys," his voice finally erupted from a roar of static, the panic in it unmistakable. "We're totally socked in here. Wind at fifty and sixty and rising. Visibility at zero." The signal died.

"Grimaldi!" Katz barked, his alarm matching the pilot's. "Come in, Grimaldi. What's wrong with your radio? Do you read me?"

"Already tried taking this crate up twice..."

the static-mashed words came. "Can't get any lift...wind keeps putting me down...nearly capsized once." Then in a clear, crisp moment of transmission, "You guys tie down there as best you can. I'll get there the minute this blows over. Take cover, do you hear? Prudhoe says it's the blizzard of the century. They are totally buried."

The signal again went weak. "Sorry, you guys...truly am. One of those freak things...nobody...could predict. Hang on...hang on...."

The copter radio went out completely; only static could be heard. Try as they might, none of the team members could raise Grimaldi.

Katz clicked off his walkie-talkie, turned to the others, his eyes haunted. "The blizzard of the century," he muttered. "And we're a hundred miles from nowhere."

8

For long moments no member of Phoenix Force uttered a word. Deliberately they avoided looking at each other, none wanting the other to read the despair reflected in his eyes. What now? Huddle behind a rock? Struggle to keep a fire going? Even if the Arctic fury permitted it, how long would that last? They would be turned into ice statues within an hour.

It would constitute the ultimate practical joke. They had faced down every danger the world's most ruthless terrorists could throw at them. Bullets, grenades, knives, demolition blasts— terror beneath and above the sea. Then, to buy it this way.... To run in circles against the one enemy too big to handle. To be turned into large, economy-sized ice cubes.

"Can we gather some branches?" Encizo finally offered. "Build a lean-to of some sort?"

"Never work," McCarter said. "We'd just take a little longer to freeze, that's all."

It was then they noticed that Gary Manning was gone. Searching the shrieking, shifting walls of snow, they saw no sign of him. The wind actually took Keio's legs out from under him, and he clawed for a fingerhold against its terrifying force.

"Gary," Encizo howled helplessly against the storm. "Where are you? Get your ass back here. This is no time to be wandering off. Manning, do you hear me?"

The wind whipped away the useless shouts, his outcry barely registering three feet away.

Before the rest could take up with bellowings of their own, a dim shape solidified in the snow, and they saw Manning, an improvised sounding pole in his hands. They watched in bafflement as he poked it into the snow again and again.

"What in hell?" McCarter challenged. "What're you doing, mate?"

"Looking for snow."

"Looking for snow?" McCarter screamed. "You dumb Canuck, there's a million miles of it all around us."

"The right kind of snow," Manning called back. "Leave me be. The rest of you draw up the Finncats. Make a semicircle to the north of me, form a windbreak of sorts." He drove the probe into the snow a last time. "Here," he urged. "This feels right to me."

By the time the snowmobiles were coaxed back to life, herded into tight revetment, Manning was studiously pacing a twelve-foot circle in the snow, stamping on the hard-packed crust that had been building in the Arctic since early November. "Keio," he commanded, "that funny looking knife in the boot you were asking about before. Bring it."

The Canadian's sense of urgency was infectious, and the rest of the men gathered close, curious about Manning's behavior.

"Gary," Katz insisted, "what are you doing?"

"An igloo," he replied tersely, taking the knife—thin, razor sharp, over a foot long—from the scabbard that Keio now thrust into his hands. "It's our only chance."

"An igloo?" Yakov gaped. "You know how to build one?"

"I did once. Just pray I haven't forgotten how." Instantly he leaned forward, slashed the knife into the wind-packed snow. A moment later he sawed into the crust and brought up a block of snow that was fourteen by fourteen, at least a foot thick.

"An igloo?" McCarter scoffed. "You're crazy, man. That'll take all day. We'll be frozen solid by then."

"You got any better ideas?" Manning snapped, the knife flashing as it shaped the snow block to precise bias on both bearing edges. "You gonna stand there yammering, or you going to help?"

"Sure thing, mate," McCarter said. "Just tell me what to do."

"Get those packing tarps out of the Finncats," he urged. "Gather them in one place. Get the weapons under cover and any food we've got left, those aluminum containers it came in.... There should be some sterno stuff in those kits. I know there's a Hank Roberts stove-lantern in mine. Get ready for a bit of hibernation, my friend."

And to Rafael he said, "Place the blocks as I dig them. Butt them as tight as you can." The knife never stopped, and shortly four ice cakes were lying on the outer rim of the ring he was rapidly digging himself into.

The first blocks were cut on gradual incline, like a circular ramp. Later they were cut to uniform size, the cant thus produced giving the courses a spiraling configuration. Special taper was given to each succeeding block so the igloo dome gradually began to form.

An unshaped block of snow was flung to the Israeli. "Katz, stamp that to powder, fill in the cracks as we go."

Keio Ohara disappeared briefly and returned with a knife of his own—an "Arkansas toothpick," its blade twelve inches long. "Picked this up at a flea market." He smiled shyly. "Just tell me how you want them cut, Gary."

Moments later blocks of compressed snow were peppering the crusted snowfield, Manning grumbling to himself as he was forced to recut them two and three times to give them correct slant. He was rusty, but his proficiency slowly returned as the haphazard construction went on. Keio, too, caught on fast, doing the rough cuts, giving them to Manning for precise trimming.

And though the blizzard continued to build, the piercing wind almost sucking their breath away at times, turning the men's face masks to sheet ice, they hardly noticed. Racing against time, fired by the urgency of their task, they worked like men possessed.

Little by little the circle of inward-leaning ice blocks mounted. One course high, then two. Then a whole section of the third course collapsed. A flurry of groans and curses carried as all joined to repair the damage. Several blocks split, partially disintegrated, and new ones had to be cut.

"Goddamn," Encizo roared as the wind hit him like sheets of plywood slamming against his body. "How can it be so cold and not freeze solid?"

While they worked, Manning explained that one October during a hunting expedition to Great Bear Lake, his party had been caught by a freak storm, and their Eskimo guides had erected an emergency igloo. Manning had pitched in, learning his basic skills then and there. Later he had researched Arctic survival techniques.

"This is going to be one helluva excuse for an igloo," he apologized. "But it'll have to do."

Another frantic hour later, all hands chilled to the bone, limbs and fingers leaden, all wondering if they could hold out another fifteen minutes, they were putting finishing touches on the ice dome. Manning and Keio worked inside by an emergency flashlight, while the rest continued shoring up the outside with snow, throwing it up at the igloo, molding a second reinforcing layer, stuffing every crack. The peak was particularly troublesome, and caved in twice before the king block was finally in place. Manning deftly opened an air hole with his knife.

The entrance tunnel—*tor-sho*, according to the Eskimo—was makeshift, no more than a trench leading to the doorway, covered over with slabs of snow. It faced away from the direction of the wind. A double slab of snow blocks waited inside the door for the time when everyone was inside.

It was now 1430 hours, the blizzard howling with even more demonic fury. "Last call," Manning announced with a self-satisfied smile. "Check those vehicles for anything you might need, guys. Anybody need to use the litter box? Now or never. We dig a hole in the floor once we get locked in."

Encizo, wheezing and complaining, crawling down the tunnel on all fours, was last man in.

Manning fitted the double layer over the opening and plugged the edges with snow.

For the next ten minutes all five men performed a crouched shuffle inside to tamp down the snow. Next the tarps were spread out like primitive carpeting. At last the team sprawled upon the floor, on the verge of exhaustion.

An eerie silence fell upon them. Listening to the muffled wail of the wind as it hit the igloo with slapping impact, they sensed an inviolable bond of camaraderie. Once again, acting as a team, drawing on inner resources, they had cheated death. The feeling of union was almost a tangible thing, and as they exchanged guarded looks, each man smiled foolishly.

"Here's to hell," Encizo intoned.

"And all her ugly little children." Keio Ohara provided the refrain.

"And here's to Gary," Yakov muttered, his eyes shining with new respect. "I'm very glad he goes hunting with Eskimos."

"Our goose would've been cooked for sure," McCarter said. "Frozen, I mean. Good show, mate. God almighty, but it's good to be outta that wind."

"What about air?" Rafael said. "Any chance of suffocating in here?"

Manning looked up at the hole in the ceiling, through which snow randomly sifted down. "No way."

The temperature in the igloo stood at zero. But to Phoenix Force, after the winter onslaught outside, it seemed almost tropical. "It'll get up to forty, fifty in time," Manning explained. "With body heat and the stoves, we'll be warm enough."

Keio sighed, huddling his face against his knees. His face mask off, his parka half open, he looked haggard.

A fresh slap of wind hit the igloo. "Any chance the storm will cave us in?" Yakov asked.

"Hardly. The Eskimos use these up by Baffin Bay, where the wind hits a hundred miles an hour." Manning smiled. "Later, as the heat builds, the moisture will glaze the walls. That'll reinforce things."

Yakov was busy with the radio again, trying to inform Grimaldi of the situation. But still there was nothing except hard, hissing static.

Another long silence followed, each man lost in

solitary thoughts, savoring the return of feeling to chilled faces and hands. There was worry as well.

"How long, Yakov?" McCarter finally said. "The storm, I mean."

"Hard to tell. It could be a couple of days or a couple hours. I'd estimate we'll be here overnight at any rate."

Abruptly Yakov clicked off the emergency light, throwing the igloo into total darkness. "We'd best conserve our resources. We've got a long night ahead of us. We'll fire up the Hank Roberts later, do some cooking. I suggest that for now we bundle up, kill time with a little sleep."

"Good idea," Manning grunted, falling back onto his tarp, drawing his hood about his face. "I'm beat."

There were guttural sighs, sounds of cartridge belts dropping, of men adjusting their cold-weather suits. "Anyone want to borrow a hand warmer?" Encizo offered. "Got an extra."

"Not me," Keio said. "Mine's still perking."

There was silence then, only the howls of the wind to be heard in the igloo's cramped confines. Soon Yakov began to snore.

Outside, the Arctic fury built up.

AT THAT SAME MOMENT, the afternoon waning, the complement at QSS 0022 was similarly confined to quarters. With one marked difference, however— surrounded by the comparative luxury the USAF facility afforded, they could endure the snowed-in conditions with considerably more forbearance than the men of Phoenix Force.

In Sean Toolan's quarters, Toolan and Mike Kelsay were involved in a war council of sorts, with Toolan already enjoined upon the day's drinking, his coherence partially undermined. "I'm worried," he said. "All these delays and that damned Avancini putting me off and all. We should never have come. Smelling the bloody stench of death, I am."

"What can we do, Sean, the weather being what it is?" Kelsay asked. Following the disastrous probe mission near Toolik two days back, and the loss of Bryan Cafferty and the rest, Kelsay had become second-in-command. It was, to his mind, a dubious promotion at best.

"I've got a broodin' in me gut, lad," Toolan went on. "Ever since Bryan cashed in. Him taking my gun and all. It's an omen, or I miss my bet. I've had that Sten since 1975. It was my lucky charm." He sipped at his whiskey and made a wry face. "No good will be coming of it, mark me. And who was it, I ask you? Who did such ugly work on our boys? You were there, Michael."

"Like I've said before, Sean. I can't tell you. That helicopter came down all of a sudden, and we had to clear away. I saw some men in white. How many, whether they were Army people or not, I can't say. That damned squall comin' up just then. I waited till there was no more shooting, then I got out. We couldn't be risking our own aircraft now, could we?"

"It was that same crew that wrecked us in Seattle, I'm thinking. But who are they? What's their place in all this? Avancini is trying to find out for us. He says he's seen them prowlin' about at Prudhoe. An inspection team, my foot. Jesus, Mary and Joseph. If I once get my hands on those bastards...."

The phone on Lieutenant Pollard's desk rang. It was Tom Lynch, manning the security watch in the com section. "Sean? I've got our man on the line. He wishes a word with you."

Toolan frowned as the connection was completed. "Well," he greeted snidely, "speak of the devil. What word, mate?"

"I'll be brief," Avancini said, "before someone finds me on this line. We can't delay much longer. You and your men have to move soon. I've done all I can do here. Everything's in place for the strike. It's your turn now."

"And what should I be doing, do you suppose? With these damned blizzards every half hour."

"Sunday night," the contact man insisted. "Weather permitting. According to plan. Security's loosening up here again. All arrangements are on schedule. If the storm doesn't lift, then the next day. I'll be in touch, of course."

"And our commando friends? What do we do about them?"

Avancini chuckled malevolently. "We won't be hearing from them again. Last report has them lost out in the snow somewhere. Entirely cut off.

They won't survive the night. Wolf food, come thaw time.''

Toolan's smile was gleeful. "That *is* good news. Makes me feel that much better about Sunday. It *is* a night strike, isn't it?"

"I said, according to plan," the traitor snapped. "Why don't you take an ad in the paper?"

"Just checking. Don't go gettin' huffed. Sunday night then."

End of communication. Toolan regarded the dead phone bemusedly. "Sunday night it is, Michael," he said, reaching for the bottle. "That calls for a drink, wouldn't you say?" They raised their glasses. "*Salud* and *slainte*," Sean toasted.

IN STILL ANOTHER PART of the Satellite Control Facility, in a dimly lit room at the furthermost end of the corridor, there was a parlay of quite a different kind.

"No, Clancy," Coletta Devane giggled, well jarred herself. "Such a pig-ignorant sod you are. Clothes off, damn you. I ain't screwin' any man with buttons to scratch and all. Get that shirt off, do you hear?"

"But what if Sean should come along?" Clancy Dolan said. "And catch me and Derwin with you? He'll be killing us by inches."

"The hell with Sean Toolan," the woman said, her eyes glowing. "He don't give a pig's tit what I do, or who I do it with."

Close to fulfillment of two driving urges—to avenge herself upon an indifferent lover and to experience tandem sex once in her life—she was impatient with her overly modest partner. Derwin McSherry, his head already berthed between her silky thighs, was breathing hard.

Dolan swiftly removed the rest of his clothes and approached the bed.

"Now isn't that the sweetest lad?" the woman sighed, her eyes intent on his lower body.

Dolan arranged himself high upon her torso.

SOMEHOW THE DAY HAD PASSED, and now, at 0100 hours, the men of Phoenix Force were stirring restlessly. The Hank Roberts stove-lantern hissed softly, the second container of LP butane in place. McCarter shifted to avoid a persistent drip where the heat buildup melted the snow.

Outside the wind still whistled and howled.

"I think we're completely buried," Keio murmured. "The wind seems more muffled. Any danger?"

Manning's eyes went to the dome. "Not so long as our little blowhole is open."

"I would never have believed it'd get this warm," McCarter muttered.

"Eskimo babies run around nude in these things once they get things balanced," Manning said. "When they settle in for a week or so at a stretch."

"I'll pass on that." McCarter grimaced. "I'd go stir crazy. I feel like I've been in here for a month already. The smell alone. But what're you gonna do? We damned sure can't go outside." He winked. "An insult to my natural modesty."

"That'll be the day," Keio teased.

Again the men fell silent. The dim glow from the stove caught their faces in ruddy outline, emphasizing the hard, shadowed planes of cheekbones and brows, the grim determination of their mouths. Rugged bodies, used to hard action, did not respond kindly to cramped, enforced inactivity. Neither did take-charge mentalities.

In his area, Rafael Encizo was not sleeping. Eyes blank, he was thinking grim thoughts, his mind going back to another time in his life when he had been similarly caged.

Only worse.

Once more he was back in the reeking dungeons of Castro's El Principe prison. There had been stench there too, life being lived at its rawest, most elemental level. The slop pails were always full to overflowing, men actually voiding on the dirt floors when dysentery and rotten food robbed them of even that final dignity.

He recalled the moans and shrieks in the night, a carry-over from the day's torture sessions. Fidel's bullyboys had sat up nights devising sadistic innovations. He recalled the dark hours when men had pleaded with their cellmates to kill them, put them out of their misery.

Even more galling, Rafael remembered how—when his escape plans were finalized—he could get none of his cellmates to make the break with him. Terrified, weak, spineless, they chose to cower where they were; freedom was a distant, glittering chimera, impossible to attain.

The chilling analogy between that time and his present circumstances was an easy leap. Again he was imprisoned, but with an important difference: here he was with comrades who would back him to the hilt, who were willing to risk all. To them freedom was not a dream, it was gut-level stuff, within reach. But you had to pursue it, fight for it. It was what their lives, what Phoenix Force was all about.

Down the line McCarter sighed heavily. "Isn't this bloody storm ever going to blow over?"

Nobody dignified the question with a reply.

The aura of surrealistic timelessness deepened. Aggravation mounted, a hair-trigger tension infecting each man. They were encased in a brooding cocoon, each man isolated from his mates. Private thoughts of vengeance. Doomful, black thoughts.

Thoughts of Grey Dog. And an impending showdown.

The endless vigil went on.

And still the blizzard gave no sign of letting up.

9

Some time around 0600 hours the storm finally began to abate. They awoke from a cramped, restless sleep, and were awed by the eerie silence surrounding them. Each man looked about in the suffocating darkness, hardly able to believe his ears.

"Man," McCarter exclaimed, "that's bloody spooky. After all that racket." He struggled to his feet. "I'm gettin' my ass outta here."

"Stay where you are," Yakov ordered. "What good are you going to do out there? Grimaldi will be out looking for us as soon as he possibly can."

Yakov busied himself with the radio. But again no amount of adjustment would bring in anything other than static. "If I could just let him know we're all right," he fussed. "I'll bet he's worrying himself sick." Then to Manning he said, "Did you remember the flare pistol? When and if he does fly over?"

"Check," Manning responded.

At 0815 hours they heard the muffled clatter of the Bell Long Ranger's rotors overhead. Manning went to the igloo's center, poked the barrel of the Very pistol out of the air hole and jerked the trigger. Moments later there was a flat report, and suddenly the night went red. Immediately the patrolling chopper doubled back.

"Pack up, everybody," Encizo called in playful falsetto. "Today we go home from camp."

One by one the Phoenix members burrowed their way out of the snowed-in tunnel, emerging spluttering and gasping. As Yakov, the last to emerge, appeared, Grimaldi was coming across the opening, up to his waist in snow. He embraced Manning, then Katzenelenbogen, clapping them heartily on the shoulder. "If you bastards ain't a sight for sore eyes," he greeted, his voice husky with emotion. "I thought you were goners for sure."

For long moments Grimaldi stood admiring what could be seen of the igloo. "Well I'll be damned," he said. "Leave it to you guys."

Rafael draped his arm over Manning's shoulder. "Our scoutmaster," he joked.

By 1115 hours, showered and shaved, a hearty breakfast put away, wearing fresh issue of clothing, all hands were closeted with Clark Jessup, the Stony Man-Pentagon liaison, for an update and strategy briefing. Also included in the meeting was Major Sam Harrington, the Prudhoe front man and procurement officer with whom they had worked ever since arriving.

Jessup came directly to the point. "Where in hell are the Irish terrorists?" he blustered, scowling angrily. "Are we chasing our goddamned tails or what?"

"Your guess is as good as mine," Katzenelen-bogen said, bristling a little at the bureaucrat's implication that they were bungling the mission. "One thing is certain: they aren't where we've been looking."

"So?"

"We have to start looking somewhere else."

"And where might that somewhere be?"

Katz patiently described the scope of their search to the officious Defense Department representative, managing to conceal the rancor he was feeling. He filled Jessup in on the zilch mission just completed, adding that further low-level reconnaissance on their way back to Prudhoe had also uncovered nothing. If they thought that the fresh dusting of snow would reveal Grey Dog tracks, they were mistaken.

"The whole line, all the way from Toolik to Prudhoe," Yakov concluded sourly, "was clean." He ducked his head defensively. "I was wrong. I was sure they were there. Which means I must totally revamp my thinking. That's why I've invited Major Harrington here; he knows the North Slope like the back of his hand. Perhaps he can provide us with some more constructive leads."

Jessup frowned and turned to Harrington. "What've you got, Sam?"

Harrington had sheafs of topographicals pinpointing every station, construction site, supply camp, isolated village and landfill within a two-hundred-mile range of Prudhoe—most of which Mack Bolan's crack team had already considered.

Which brought them back to square one.

"False leads, every one," Yakov said. "So you tell me. Where do we look? They sure as hell aren't flying back to Ireland every night."

"These designations here," Keio broke in, stabbing the map with a finger, "what are they?"

"Those are major and minor BMEWS stations in our Space Defense System," Harrington explained. "Ballistic missile early-warning system."

"And this one here, near the Colville River?" Keio persisted. "It's within helicopter range of the pipeline."

"That's QSS 0022."

"QSS 0022?"

"Yes," Harrington said, a touch of reticence in his answer. "Top-secret stuff. Satellite Control Facility. It's a global network to keep tabs on position and status of all satellites, our own as well as those the Russians send up." His tone turned condescending. "What're you getting at? Surely you aren't suggesting that.... Oh, no, that's impossible."

"Is it?" Keio's stare was harsh, unflinching. "It seems to me that it would be a perfect setup."

Instant silence hit as the startling conjecture sank in. "Good God!" Yakov exclaimed. "Could it be? How could we be so stupid?"

"Impossible," Harrington repeated. "These stations are reporting in around the clock. They have fantastic security and communication clearance. Our monitors would spot a takeover within minutes."

"Would they?" the Japanese martial arts expert challenged. "Security codes have been circumvented before. We shouldn't underestimate the terrorist networks."

Katz provided a quick overview of the Jeddah-Red Bluff Arsenal caper, in which Red Anvil, an Arab terrorist group, had infiltrated key military nerve centers worldwide, months prior to the scheduled strike. "It could just as easily be taking place at QSS 0022," he concluded.

"Well, there sure as hell is a quick way to find out. I'll call intelligence at Eileson AFB. They have jurisdiction. They'll certainly know if anything's fishy." He rose. "I'll have to use a secure line. If you'll excuse me."

"A suggestion, Major," Yakov said. "Please have your man put the reporting technician at the satellite base to the wall. Discreetly, of course, so they won't suspect we're digging. Keep them on the horn as long as possible."

"Can do, Colonel."

Harrington was gone for fifteen minutes. When he returned his face was pale, the sick, dismayed expression telegraphing his findings before he spoke a word.

"They're there," he said. "No doubt about it. I was patched in, heard the whole thing. They were not giving the right answers. It's obvious someone was holding a gun to the man's head. The chief could not be contacted, which is a prime security breach in itself."

Harrington directed an apologetic smile to

Keio, respect in his eyes. "You were right," he said. "How'd you ever stumble on that one...."

Keio flushed and made no reply save for a shy grin.

"So?" Jessup interrupted. "Where do we go from here?"

It was without question, Harrington declared, a hostage situation. "Which means we can't go in at company strength." He sighed, his eyes bleak. "It would mean wholesale slaughter."

He looked at Katz. "Do you think, under the circumstances...you and your men could get in with minimum losses? Once we rescue our personnel we throw everything we've got against them."

Katz sent him an arch look. "You make it sound so easy." He lapsed into thought, his steel hooks clicking steadily. "It could be done. Commando stuff...that's our line. You're positive your contact didn't wake any sleeping dogs there?"

"I'm sure, Colonel. He was one sharp operator."

"What about air traffic? Will we arouse suspicion if we fly over later, get the lie of the land?"

"This is still Alaska," Harrington said. "Air traffic is constant. Recon to your heart's content. Nobody will give you a second look."

"Have your people do a rush maintenance on the Bell we've been using. We'll aim for a 1330 hours liftoff." He stood. "Gentlemen."

Phoenix Force rose as one man. A new, purposeful confidence reborn within them, they left

the office in long, rapid strides, their faces gone
hard.

By 1445 hours they were homing on the Satellite
Control Facility, Jack Grimaldi pushing the Bell
Long Ranger hard. When they were twenty miles
out, Katz ordered him to throttle down and drop
the bird to two hundred, then one hundred feet
above ground. Visibility poor as usual, they took
pains to pinpoint landmarks that would later lead
them in.

Tomorrow night they would approach overland, using the Finncats that the Army was retriev-
ing from the site of their igloo. When they came
within two miles of QSS 0022, they would continue the rest of the way on skis. And from there
on in. . . play it by ear.

"Good hardpack here," Katz said. "We'll set
down now, do our unloading. That long outcropping of rock there. Like an arrow almost. It'll lead
us in. An eight-mile jump at best. . . ."

"Right on, chief. Got a fix," Grimaldi said, excitement shading his tones. Moonlight on the killing ground, he mused.

Shortly they closed on the installation, Grimaldi
being careful not to fly in too slowly and draw the
enemy's attention. Each man was silent, intent on
the eerie scene below.

They were struck by the disarming peacefulness
of the scene. The long snow-covered buildings, the
banks of radar shields, the radar dishes surrounding the entire facility, all were taken into con-
sideration. A helicopter hangar stood about a

hundred yards from the facility proper. In the floodlit yard stood a jeep, two half-ton trucks, and a Caterpillar tractor rigged with an eight-foot snowblade. The copter pad and an abbreviated landing strip to the west were plowed clean, the drifts at least fifteen feet high along the edges.

More impressive were the observation domes.

Equally unsettling was the total lack of activity at the station. It gave the impression of being totally deserted.

The men studied the layout of the base, noting door locations, distances involved in getting from one building to the other, from the base to the huge aircraft hangar. "I only see two main doors," Yakov commented, consulting the blueprints that Harrington had provided earlier. "Plus the loading bays." He marked on the blueprint the doors that were blocked with snow.

"A double-pronged attack, I'd say," he went on. "Encizo and Ohara will take this one. The rest of us will come into the dome areas proper."

Grimaldi executed two more passes over the installation. "Got it, gang?" he asked. "Let's not push our luck too far."

Katz nodded and gestured for Grimaldi to take on some sky. The Bell edged off gradually, lifting in a slow climb.

Tension inside the cabin was thick; it could seemingly be sectioned with a knife. As they put distance between themselves and QSS 0022, the men's minds were already racing, inventorying weapons, envisioning the attack. After so many false leads....

It was time.

"When's splashdown, Yakov?" McCarter broke the silence.

"Approximately 2300 hours tomorrow night. We'll need extra time to coordinate things. You know how the government works. S-l-o-w."

He frowned. "The Grey Dog people will most likely be sacked in by then, with just a skeleton crew on duty. With any luck they'll confine the GIs to one area. If we can isolate that sector, then move on out from there.... Strictly hand to hand, gentlemen. Until we're sure the Americans are safe."

McCarter chortled to himself. "After that we shoot out their eyes."

The copter picked up speed and raced toward Prudhoe Bay.

10

The unloading of the Sikorsky S-65 was completed with speed. The temperature standing at thirty below, a ten-mile jaunt across frigid terrain ahead of them, Phoenix Force was in no mood for delay. The wind, tame as it was, still cut at exposed skin like a million razors.

As before, Grimaldi and the Sikorsky crew were put on standby. Loose radio contact would be maintained.

Tonight no headlights were allowed on the Finncats. Yakov and Rafael rode at the head of the column, Keio and McCarter behind, with Manning bringing up the rear. The snow vehicles sliced smoothly through the night, the tracks skimming the hardpan at an even forty. Ahead of Phoenix Force, as far as the eye could see, the ocean of snow glistened with a dull sheen where the starshine reflected on it. Here and there black outcroppings of rock loomed ominously against the ice prairie.

Each man carried an Ingram MAC-10, his cartridge belt festooned with as many magazines as he could carry, as well as an assortment of M-26 fragmentation grenades. The Ingram had been chosen for its proven superiority in close fighting situations.

Also, assorted personal weapons were leathered inside the cold-weather suits. Gary Manning carried his usual, the .44 AutoMag, which was Mack Bolan's favorite convincer. Rafael Encizo had tucked a .380 Walther PPK close to his heart; his Gerber Mark I survival knife was stored in a specially made sheath at the small of his back. Keio Ohara also chose the heavyweight AutoMag. In addition, the "Arkansas toothpick" was strapped to one leg, his garroting silk in a convenient place inside his clothes.

Yakov Katzenelenbogen was content with an Uzi. David McCarter—who always dealt in excesses—sported a Browning Hi-Power and a Smith & Wesson .357 Magnum.

Strapped to the right side of each Finncat, between the seat and the fairing, was a pair of Head cross-country skis that Harrington had scrounged up.

It seemed they were hardly under way, becoming accustomed to the punishing cold and to the exhilarating flow and rhythm of the fleet Finncats, when Katz began easing back. A dull glow on the horizon—testament to the clarity of the air—told them the satellite tracking station was close.

Five minutes later they were heading out, the soft whish-whish of the skis hardly carrying over the haunting moan of the wind. "We'll skirt the buildings on the south," Yakov reminded them, "come in from the west—just in case there should be any guards, which I seriously doubt. These people are cocky as hell."

He keyed the Johnson 577 walkie-talkie as they advanced, the domes glowing faintly in the distance. "We're moving in, Grimaldi," he snapped. "Stand by."

"Got you, chief," came the crisp acknowledge.

The submachine guns underwent a last check, 30-round magazines of .45 caliber were eagerly slapped into place. "Geronimo time, chaps," McCarter muttered, the light from the base giving strong definition to the cruel line of his mouth. "Just let me at those sadistic degenerates."

The strike force halted as it came within a quarter mile of the station. The men watched and listened for any movement. The low-slung building, the huge half-globes were clearly visible. There was no sound. Nothing moved.

"Head out," Yakov said.

Phoenix Force flanked the dark hangar, circling in from the west. Momentarily they were awed by the hundred-foot-high radar trackers towering above them, the chatter and scream of the wind in the steel superstructure setting nerves on edge. They worked their way down a mild grade, emerging behind the mountainous piles of snow that framed the motor pool. The skis were removed and slammed into a drift.

Hearts pumped. Adrenaline surged, breath was sucked in faster than was wise. Yakov crept forward. Gloved fingers fretted triggers nervously as he stealthily moved into the open. Only silence answered his bravado. "You know the plan," he whispered, his voice seeming to boom in the quiet. "Manning, McCarter, you come with me."

Then he charged across the parking area, his movements surprisingly agile and fluid for a man of fifty-five. Encizo and Ohara hefted their Ingrams and flung themselves left, their booted feet squeaking against the snow. As they observed Yakov at the door just beneath the main geodesic dome, and saw the door swing open at the mere turn of the knob, they slid to a stop at their assigned station.

"The morons didn't even have sense enough to lock up," Rafael grunted as they edged toward their door.

"We should be so lucky," Keio said.

And they were, the knob turning free in Rafael's palm. Inch by slow inch, his face pressed to the crack, the Cuban let it swing wider. A long corridor—apparently a billeting area—stretched before them, a red bulb at the far end providing feeble light. Swiftly, before a draft could alert the Irish hardmen, they darted inside, clicking the door shut behind them.

For long moments they remained frozen in the shadows, pressed flat against the wall. Frantic minutes were wasted peeling away face masks, opening their jump suits, pulling off gloves, waiting for gun steel to absorb some of the inner warmth. And when a testing finger failed to adhere to the trigger guard—

"Here we go," Rafael whispered.

Cursing their clumsy boots, they oozed past one closed door after another. Hearing no sound at all, they dared to press an ear to the panels, straining for the sound of snoring, muttered conversation, anything. And as door after door gave no signal of occupancy, a nagging premonition set in. What in hell was going on here?

Just then a door ahead clicked open. A man, dressed only in his skivvies, stepped into the hall. Sleep-drugged, yawning, heading for the can, he did not look back. At least not at first. But then, three steps later, he glanced sideways and got a glimpse of white-suited hulks from the corner of his eye. "Mates?" he called tentatively.

"Go," Rafael whispered, and he and Keio moved forward, taking the man before an alerting squawk could escape his lips. Black silk hissed, and even as Encizo drove his knee into the terrorist's back, wrenching his chin up, the garrote was expertly placed, twisted with merciless force.

The hardguy gagged, gurgled softly, a glottal whine managing to wedge its way through Encizo's muffling fingers. His fingers hooked and raked, seeking a last-ditch hold; his body twisted. Then, just as swiftly, all fight left him. Keio maintained the strangle-bar pressure ninety seconds longer. The man sagged to the floor, dead.

They froze again, listening, then retreated to the room the victim had just left. The door ajar, they carefully peered inside and saw no one. Hastily they retrieved the corpse and lowered it onto the bed.

Once more they worked their way forward.

Yakov's insistence that American lives be spared, if possible, buzzed in their minds—thus the mindless execution just finished. And heaven help any other Irish pigs who got in their way between here and there. Again ears were pressed to doors. Again there was not the slightest sound of human presence. The cold feeling in their gut intensified.

Then they were at the end of the hallway. A clatter around the corner put them on guard. Stealthy, fleeting recon revealed a closed, swing-type door with a single porthole in it. The galley obviously; snacks were being made for the night watch.

They crept to the door, risking glances through the window. A solitary man worked busily over a steam table. His age, his florid complexion, the ragtag clothing he wore was indication that he was no GI.

His eyes went wide with terror as a hinge-squeak alerted him, and he turned to see the white-suited figures closing on him. "God's eyes," he gasped, the brogue unmistakable. "Please now, lads...."

"Silence," Rafael whispered, "and you live. Otherwise...."

Because neither man raised his ugly Ingram chatterbox, the Grey Dog member foolishly imagined he had a chance. A furtive hand moved behind him and closed on a sharp cleaver. Borrowing bravado, the bastard's lips moved slightly, telegraphing warning of impending outcry.

Even in his cumbersome gear, Keio moved with blinding speed, a hand and foot hammering forward with pile-driver force. "Sorry, mister," he gritted, his eyes cold. A fluid side kick hit the terrorist's elbow with sledgehammer power, all but dislocating the joint. Simultaneously, suppressing the ingrained *kiai* shout, he aimed a *shuto* chop at the man's face. There was the crisp sound of bone breaking, of sloppy, tearing flesh.

Even before the miserable scum could release an agonized howl, Ohara's left hand flicked forth and pounded a *nukite* stab into his exposed throat, rupturing his epiglottis, shattering his Adam's apple. The blow crowded his windpipe with all sorts of bone and flesh. Instant suffocation.

The cook gagged hideously, his hands clutching at his throat. He fell to his knees, his eyes wide with astonished disbelief that life was ending so suddenly. He went into a terminal choke and died.

IN ANOTHER PART of the satellite tracking station, the remaining Phoenix Force members were meeting with similar puzzlement. Katz held position just outside the double doors leading into the main dome area, pondering the sparse cadre on the floor, while McCarter and Manning prowled the adjoining corridors and service areas. A skeleton crew he had expected, but this was eerie.

There were only two USAF technicians on the floor, each flanked by his own INLA watchdog. The airmen moved with a sleepwalker's gait, gliding from console to console, keeping ahead of the monitoring chores normally allotted to four men. The Irish goons were equally bored. Side arms holstered, assured by long days of guard duty that the Yanks would make no sudden moves, they were merely putting in time.

It was Katz's turn for cold chills. Where were the rest? The facility should be crawling with bodies.

Behind him, sneaking around the generator rooms, edging around piles of boxes in the storage areas, opening doors with painstaking care, the tension murderous, McCarter and Manning were finding only empty space.

"Nothing back there." Manning made a whispered report when they filtered in behind Katz. "I'm getting bad vibes."

"Me, too," said Yakov, his mouth drawn to a worried line.

Just then they heard voices and the sound of thumping boots coming from their left, from the corridor Encizo and Ohara were supposedly patrolling. Hurriedly the trio scuttled backward and eased into a cubbyhole office. Katz, his eye to the crack in the door, watched two Grey Dogs, Colt .45s on their hip, swagger into view and push their way into the control center.

"How'd our desperados miss those two?" McCarter asked.

"Hope for the best," Yakov said tersely. "I didn't hear any shooting anyway. They're waiting for an opening."

After a momentary pause they edged from their

hiding place and slid back into the corridor. Again they monitored the action.

The newcomers, dressed in fresh khakis, were sprawled in chairs, their feet up on desks, making small talk with the day shift. Apparently guard relief, they were not taking over until the clock said so. The four hardmen, wizened, wiry specimens, were arrogantly confident, never dreaming that death, bloody and violent, was only moments away.

It was then that Katz and crew heard a soft, under-the-breath whistle, carrying from their left.

"Hang tough," Katz murmured. "They're coming up."

There was an impromptu strategy session then, as Keio and Rafael emerged from the gloom. Crouched in tight huddle it was decided that, no matter what, the rest of the GIs must be found. To attack the control center without guarantee of their safety would violate iron-clad priorities. Those doors must all be cracked. If open war broke out, at least there was that chance of rescue. But the two fly-boys in the dome would become sacrificial goats.

Again Keio and Rafael, McCarter and Manning with them, faded out of sight. Katz maintained vigil outside the nerve center. "Move it," he hissed as they left. "The guards will be changing shifts any minute now."

They searched, room to room.

The snick of a latch, a pinprick of searching penlight strafing the gloom, assured that the room was unoccupied. It was as before. Nothing. A glut of bedrolls on the floor, unmade, rumpled beds, all empty. One cubicle, obviously officer country, looked like it had accommodated pigs. But the pigs were gone.

Tension gradually turned to souring despair, as room after room produced no terrorists, no U.S. troops. They concluded that they had been had.

They came upon the hardman Keio had killed, but no other bodies. Until they reached the third to last room.

Encizo stiffened, sucking in a rasping breath as he saw the grisly pileup. *"Madre de Dios!"* he groaned. *"Qué cosa?"* Instantly Keio crowded in, his light playing over the ghastly, still-life tableau.

"Filthy, rotten bastards," he said, grimacing. There were three GIs, still in their khakis, sprawled in obscene tangle on the bunks, one on the floor. Their eyes staring, last-moment supplication still registering, each lay in a thick puddle of gore, a neat third eye—dark, accusing—in the center of his forehead.

"Killed in cold blood," McCarter choked as he invaded the cramped space. He growled in barely suppressed rage. "Let's go get 'em. I'll cut out their goddamned hearts!"

But that grisly discovery was swiftly awarded second place in the shock parade upon entering the adjoining room. There they found another GI, naked this time, his uniform in disarray on the floor. He was tied in spread-eagle position on the cot. Again there was a single bullet hole in his forehead, the pillow beneath him totally saturated with blood and brain slop. Red bruises—vampire kisses—long, sweeping scratches raked his upper torso.

Scalps tightened. A rain of goose pimples fled across each man's back. Encizo's stomach tilted. "Holy God," he muttered. "I don't even wanna try guessing what this is all about."

Chilled to their souls, they reported to Katz. When he returned from the grotesque killing pens his face was dark with rage, his eyes dripped hate.

"The rest of the GIs?" Manning ventured.

"What do you think?" Katz rasped. "If they killed these poor guys...."

He fell silent, his head bowed. The men could almost hear the wheels turning in his brain. And when he finally looked up he snapped, "Rafael, you and Keio go outside. Get on that roof. Blast out part of that dome, come at them from there. The minute you open up, we'll move in down here. If we can catch them by surprise, there's a chance we can save the Americans."

"Wilco," Rafael said, immediately working to refasten his jump suit and draw up his parka. The gloves went on; the safety on his Ingram was clicked off. Shortly he and Ohara were padding down the dark corridor.

"Tear the joint down," McCarter called after them.

Inside the operational theater, the airmen sat at their consoles, shoulders hunched, expressions abject. The four Grey Dog front-liners still hung loose, joshing quietly among themselves. "There's room," Katz said softly, "if we can just blast them first."

Each man was turned into a ticking time bomb as he waited for hell to break loose inside the dome. Each yearned for the distinct privilege of being first to cut the terrorist swine to ribbons.

Just then the world exploded. An Ingram opened up on the roof, a powerhouse heel simultaneously collapsing a section of electrically heated glass. Forty-five caliber slugs rained down, turning desks, computer consoles, radar dishes to junk. The lights in the amphitheater went out momentarily, then flickered back to life.

By then, submachine guns singing a soul-satisfying death chant, Katz, McCarter and Manning were charging through the doors. They poured hot lead into the stunned enemy as the two fly-boys hit the floor, leaving them unobstructed operating room.

From above, Ohara and Encizo poured down hot death also.

With the exception of one guncock, they were all caught flat-footed; they never had time to un-holster their .45s.

McCarter whooped as he took out his man, the Ingram punching a diagonal pattern of red holes across his chest. Keio, from another angle, turned the hardguy's head to mush.

Manning sent a horizontal line of death-dealers—a quick up-and-down zip—that sliced his man wide, dropping him backward over a nearby desk.

Katz and Encizo did a job on the third guncock, their slugs hitting him hard, slamming him into a helpless spin. When he finally hit the floor, he was jetting blood like a punctured spaghetti-sauce can.

"Katz," Encizo's voice somehow carried over the earsplitting din inside the dome, "that guy on the floor. Get him. He's after the GIs."

The warning came too late. The last Irish workhorse, his shirt awash with blood, was determined to take someone with him.

Before anyone could put him down for good, the madman had emptied a full clip—seven rounds—to the spot where the airmen huddled in close knot.

McCarter came over him then. A fresh magazine in his MAC-10, he spilled all thirty rounds into the terrorist, setting his clothing to smoking, irreparably muddling his vital parts in the bargain.

They went to the GIs immediately. But the dead gunman had done his work well.

Drained, weary, a crushing sense of defeat upon them, the men of Phoenix Force stood and surveyed the havoc about them. Looking up, they saw snow drifting through the shattered part of the dome.

Their despair was interrupted by a new rattle of gunfire from outside. A second later Rafael poked his head through the dome. "We've got a live one out here, guys. Drag him in."

Where the stray Grey Dog had come from no

one ever discovered, but within sixty seconds he was inside, clutching a shattered leg, howling in agony, begging for mercy, leaking gore all over the floor.

"Mercy, is it?" McCarter taunted. "I'll give you mercy." Impatiently Yakov pushed his hot-headed mate away and tied a makeshift tourniquet around the boy's thigh.

"He was hotfooting it across the parking lot," Encizo explained.

A fierce smile on his face, the Cuban produced his Mark I and knelt close to the kid, who could not have been more than eighteen. He slid the point of the knife into the boy's left nostril, gave it a delicate twitch, cutting a precise gash in his flesh. "You're gonna tell us everything you know, aren't you?" the Cuban seethed.

As Yakov began his interrogation, and Rafael continued threatening motions with the Gerber, the terrorist commenced spilling his guts.

It was as they had thought. The main core of the INLA force—thirty-six in all—had flown the coop. They were on their way to Prudhoe. But before that there would be a series of independent strikes at the pipeline proper. They had gone in one helicopter. Takeoff time had been 2200 hours.

At that piece of information Katz slapped his forehead softly. "We probably passed them on the way. What about the other Americans?" Yakov demanded. "What about that naked man tied up in one of those rooms?"

"Outside, Captain," the yellowback babbled,

"in the snow. We killed the nine o' them our first night here."

It took all the control McCarter could master to keep from kicking the simpering swine's head to pudding.

"And the man you tortured?"

"That wasn't none o' our doing," he whined. "It was that damned Coletta Devane. She done it."

Yakov's eyes opened wide. "*She? Coletta* Devane?"

"Yeah, Sean Toolan's woman. She's got a queer streak she has. Plain daft. And just lately. . . a regular bitch in heat she's been."

The men exchanged puzzled, disbelieving glances.

"McCarter," Katz grunted, after they had pumped the turncoat for every shred of information they could get. "What should we do with him?"

The kid then reached for his only life hope—a knife in his boot.

McCarter pressed the Ingram's barrel.

The weapon bucked just once, leaving a hole big as a half dollar as it exited the other side. The terrorist went down. Nobody even bothered to look back as the boy writhed in final death throes.

Once outside, it took only a few moments to find the makeshift cemetery. And there, protruding from the snow of a compacted drift were at least eight human feet. Piled high, frozen solid, they resembled so many slabs of human meat.

Keio's lust for revenge threatened to split his brain just then. ''Those poor devils.''

Yakov was keying the walkie-talkie, his eyes feverish. ''Grimaldi,'' he barked, the urgency in his tone unmistakable. ''Come and get us. *Now*. As fast as you can make that crate go.''

11

There was no finesse to Phoenix Force's attack. Suddenly the Bell Long Ranger—transformed into a death-spitting war wagon—was dropping out of the night. They found the Grey Dog demolition team exactly where their ratchet-jawed comrade had said they would be.

One minute the Irish were operating in arrogant leisure, rigging their charges on a stretch of the Trans-Alaska Pipeline located less than two miles north of pumping station three, the next, amid the booming engine roar, the slap of rotors, the enemy was upon them. They were caught with their pants all the way to their ankles.

Before the terrorist squad could recover, the copter's spotlight pinned them in a brilliant glare, momentarily blinding them. Then, even as they tumbled off the VSLs and broke for cover, death came calling from the heavens.

Ohara, McCarter and Manning sat in the Bell's open hatch, their rifles spitting death.

One Grey Dog lay flopping at the base of a supporting trestle; another caught his death fifty feet to the right. Still another, leaving a bloody smear on the snow, crawled for an enfilade of rock on the pipe's left side.

Ingrams put aside, Phoenix Force opted for the greater range of the M-16 Keio wielded, the AK-47 McCarter was emptying, the Stoner M-63 that Manning had temporarily coaxed from Rafael. Even if the liberation army troops had had the presence of mind to try blasting the bird from the sky, they were panicked by the nonstop thunder from above, by the flat, slicing chop of hot lead at their heels as they desperately made for the high country.

Fifty minutes had passed since liftoff at QSS 0022, and now, at 2435 hours, Mack Bolan's ace avengers were coming down.

At Katzenelenbogen's direction, Grimaldi had beamed a message to Major Harrington's CQ frequency on the helicopter's radio. Flipping dials feverishly, he had been unable to raise anyone. Prudhoe was shut down, but good.

"Crap," he had groaned. "Tonight of all nights. They should be monitoring around the clock. How in hell can we warn them if nobody's on the goddamn horn?"

Keio had smiled faintly. "Could be that the fix is already in," he had said. "Somebody deliberately arranged it so nobody can get through to Prudhoe."

Faces had drawn to even sterner cast.

Flying through the frigid night, the Phoenix team had devised swift patchup to its riddled war plan. Where to hit INLA first—at Prudhoe, or at the pipeline itself? In the end the decision had been arrived at with relative ease.

Prudhoe, without a doubt, could be salvaged. Emergency crews would swarm over the base; the facility could be operational within forty-eight hours. But should the pipeline be blown in three places as the INLA rat had indicated, the damage would be irreversible. Total shutdown. In their isolated location, one hundred miles south of Prudhoe, in the dead of winter, it would take crews weeks to gear up for repairs.

By then it would be altogether too late.

On to Toolik.

Now, abruptly, the Long Ranger angled downward. As it skimmed four feet off the ground the five commandos were dropping from both sides, rolling to stand-up position, fanning out, assault rifles spattering pin-down rounds across the landscape. Encizo, again in charge of the Stoner, and Manning, fisting the CAR-15, fanned out to execute the four remaining hardmen. Behind them the others poured a withering firescreen as they raced forward in low crouch.

For his part, Grimaldi rocketed skyward as fast as he could fling levers, taking no chances of drawing a crippling round.

Manning windmilled an M-26 against the night. Again the shearing, flat whump. Again the shrill scream sounded from behind the outcropping as the wounded terror goon headed off toward death.

To the east, cowering behind rocks, stunted

pine and tamarack, the three remaining terrorists opened up with their stolen M-16s, virtually begging for instant death. Phoenix Force chewed snow, crawling forward on their bellies, each man wild to be the first to send the rats into their final rag-doll jig. Keio, in a flamboyant gesture, came to full height and whizzed two more grenades up the incline.

One bastard bailed out from behind his tree and began rolling down the hill, his bloody back making a dotted-line pattern in the snow. The others panicked, broke from cover and began crashing deeper into the woods.

As if on a pull string, Phoenix rose en masse and opened up, cartridges flying like brass birds at the edges of their vision. The terrorists stopped suddenly, bouncing back, as if they had slammed into a wall. Arms flew up at cockeyed, fractured angles; M-16s were flung high over their heads. They performed brief death dances in the snow and went down for good, their clothes spouting blood in a dozen places at once.

The five men of Phoenix took inventory. Six men at the first dropoff, the kid had said. They counted methodically.

Six, exactly.

As they slogged back down the hill, waving Grimaldi down, Keio shouted from the left flank. "Hey, take a look at this."

"I'll be goddamned." Encizo sighed. "Is this an inside job, or is this an inside job? Talk about organized."

The wide, deep gashes in the snow were unmistakable. Two tracked vehicles had been dropped in beforehand. Both were long gone—loaded with Grey Dogs—and speeding toward the next strike zones.

"M113s," Yakov said, respect for their adversaries building within him, "or I miss my bet. That kid never mentioned this."

"How in hell did they get them out here without anyone at Prudhoe getting suspicious?" McCarter asked.

"It all falls into place, doesn't it?" Keio replied. "Complete infiltration of the chain of command. A man who knows the top man. The APCs came in on sky cranes. All properly manifested, of course."

They stood in a disgruntled huddle, out of range of the Bell's rotorwash, while Manning scrambled up the VSMs, expertly dismantling the demolition setup.

"Enough C-3 there to blow up two pipelines," he reported. "From all indications, they weren't going to detonate immediately. Which suggests a domino effect, from Prudhoe on down the line."

"Maybe we've still got a chance," Yakov muttered. "Although time's running out on us."

"So?" Rafael said, his voice expectant, hoping against hope. "What now?"

"Mount up," Katz snapped. "Head them off if we can."

It was as they moved toward the chopper that Encizo suddenly stopped in his tracks, clapped his hand to his forehead. "I'll be damned," he exclaimed.

"Rafael?" Katz said, concerned. "What is it?"

"Just in case none of you noticed...." He grinned playfully. "We just missed New Year's Eve. Happy New Year, guys."

Nobody answered at first. Faces bleak, the irony of the reminder registered strongly.

"Yeah," Manning said finally, his voice flawed. "Happy New Year."

Moments later the Phoenix express was again airborne, Grimaldi skimming the pipeline at one hundred twenty miles per hour, holding at a hundred-foot elevation. Heading due north. Six sets of eyes scoured the ground beneath, six mouths cursed the damnable visibility as random sheets of ground fog made things even more soupy.

Then, suddenly, almost too late....

Their stomachs were left at elevation one hundred, each man clawing at the cabin fixtures for balance as Grimaldi shot the Bell up with sickening swiftness. "They spotted us," he rasped. "That's fifty-caliber ammo coming up. Another two seconds and they'd have zapped us for sure."

Reaching four thousand feet, safely out of range of the superpowered Browning M-2, Grimaldi leveled off and commenced circling the area where the APC had hunkered down. From that height there was no way to tell what the INLA hardmen were up to. They could operate with total impunity with armor like the Browning at their backs.

"What now, coach?" Rafael confronted Yakov, his teeth clenched in rage. "We've got nothing that can touch that."

"Haven't we?" Manning challenged, emerging from the back of the cabin, a long, blanket-wrapped cylinder braced in his hands. "Remember this baby?"

It was the Dragon M-47, the antitank weapon that, when selected earlier by Manning for inclusion in their arsenal, all had derided. "Set us down a mile ahead of that personnel carrier," he told Grimaldi. "We'll come in overland, catch them by surprise. Once I lock the sight on that baby buggy, there's no way in hell the missile can go astray. Goodbye armor plate."

Spirits revived. And as Grimaldi swung wide and began dropping, they reloaded the rifles, restocked ammo on their cartridge belts. Encizo brought forward two of the six missiles stacked in the back, the armor-piercing shell in convenient carrying pack. "Those bastards'll never know what hit 'em," he chortled.

Again Phoenix was on the snowfield, Grimaldi jetting up immediately, prowling nonstop to keep the enemy off balance. There was a mile and a half between them and the APC—a mile before they would actually set up for the missile strike—and they set out gamely, moving as fast as the paralyzing cold could allow.

Finally, the M113 only a black blur in the gloom, the Irish terrorists otherwise invisible, Manning and Encizo began to set up. The missile in the chamber, the nose tripod set up, Manning seated in the snow, bracing his body with cocked knees, they ran a quick dry run. Then they waved Yakov, Keio and McCarter away. They would be flanking to the south, ready to do a pincer the minute the missile homed in on the APC. "Give us five," Yakov called, "to sneak up on them."

"Wilco," Manning said, snugging his eyes into the sensoring scope, bringing the armored vehicle into greater magnification. "Looks like a box car," he gloated. "Can't miss from here."

"If you do," Rafael grinned, patting the carrier, "backup."

And when the allotted lead time had passed, Manning depressed the trigger, sending the gyro into spin. The gas generator booted the missile.

The rear muzzle exploded with a dull roar, belching flame and debris behind Manning's shoulder. A smoke ring flared briefly at the front end, momentarily blinding him. As quickly as it dissipated, the rocket was zooming off in flat trajectory at 250 miles per hour. From his vantage point Encizo could watch the missile in flight. Its aim electronically monitored by the sighting device, it moved unerringly on target.

Seconds later, there was an earsplitting blast as the 5.4-pound warhead connected directly amidships, bored through the 1.6-inch armor and tore the APC's guts to shreds. Everything was blown sky-high—gunner, gunner's mate, the Browning .50 caliber, and the diesel fuel in the bargain.

As the APC exploded, the night was pushed back by a crimson sunburst that fixed the Irishmen—Phoenix as well—in dazzling definition.

Hard on the terrorists' left, rifles singing a bloody kill-song, the flank party closed in. The Dragon M-47 set aside, his CAR-15 hammering, Manning also charged, using the burning tank for cover. Rafael slogged to his right, the Stoner in baying throb—the hounds of hell unleashed all at the same time.

The terrorists did not have a chance.

Bloody, flesh-disintegrating death, chunks of human meat flung heedlessly into the snow. One man, his head nearly severed, hanging by mere tendons, still stomped aimlessly in the snow for a few drunken steps before he collapsed. Another gathered himself into fetal position, gurgled hysterically, fighting to keep his intestines from spreading all over the ice. The other two resembled foundering, bloody blubber.

Two men blown to hell by the Dragon's missile, the other four caught in charnel-house cross fire, it was no contest.

Again there were no backward looks—only a headlong rush to load into the already-settling Bell Long Ranger, Manning and Encizo stopping first to recover the M-47 gear. The firing tube was discarded; the sensor-firing device swiftly clapped onto the next missile launcher.

They caught the second tracked vehicle on the move. The chopper's racket was drowned out by the growl of the M113's diesels. It was a mere matter of setting down into a convenient swale and waiting for the poor suckers to come into range. A veteran cannoneer, Manning smiled coldly, set the scope's cross hairs and waited for the vehicle to come closer, still closer.

And as it came over a rise....

Again the flashback, the dull rumble and swoosh, the slow trip down the line. His face a study in concentration, Manning tracked the moving target expertly, deliberately locking on the driver's cockpit.

The night detonated in a frenzy of fire, blood and death. Once more it was instant slaughterhouse, bodies arcing across the horizon like human cannonballs. Those unlucky enough to miss the ride were turned to greasy barbecue in seconds flat. Somehow one patriot managed to escape the inferno, and ran screaming across the snow, his clothes on fire. Katz raised his Uzi and put the human torch out of his misery.

The five men stood watching the carnage, the raging firestorm highlighting their features, capturing the hard light in their eyes as they watched the enemy so satisfyingly sent to hell.

Then, abruptly, the blocks of C-3 in the compartments were triggered by exploding rounds. They began ripping the night with ground-jarring concussion, sending steel screaming over their heads.

Phoenix Force broke for the helicopter, climbed

aboard in pell-mell rush. Grimaldi quickly jacked the bird out of danger.

"Driver," McCarter said the minute the side hatch was secured, "take us to Prudhoe, please." And they were off.

12

At 0215 hours the emergency circuits—hotline from Valdez—flashed red in both of Prudhoe's master-operations control centers. And when, after five minutes, neither phone was picked up, the automatic override was activated.

"All personnel," the speakers surrounding the nerve centers blasted. "We are registering unauthorized entry at Valdez. Repeat, unauthorized entry. The oil-movements control center has been sabotaged. All computer systems have been destroyed. We are zero functional here. Repeat, zero functional. Alternate control position must be instituted immediately. Directive 32-A supersedes all previous instructions."

Shortly the voice became even more panicky. "We have two fatalities here. Security forces are closing in on a three-man terrorist team. Come in, Prudhoe, do you read me? Prudhoe...."

But there was no reply. There would be no reply. Because there was no personnel on hand to make a reply.

For, at that same moment, Prudhoe itself was first awakening to the fact that it too was under siege.

DROPPING ONTO the pumping station one airstrip at 0130 hours, the Boeing-Vertol CH 47C had received priority clearance from control. And when the eighteen armed men had debarked in leisurely fashion, all dressed in U.S. Air Force winter gear, all suspicion regarding their middle-of-the-night arrival was promptly allayed. It was well established that station one was observing security alert; these troops could be nothing other than reinforcement of the Army detachment already cluttering up the perimeters.

Then, when the party was greeted by Captain Dan Murray, who smilingly led them onto the heated bus that would carry them the half mile to the station proper, the bored traffic controllers did an instant brain wipe. Kin folk, and let it go at that.

It was the same with the sleepy-eyed GIs standing guard at the pumping station entrances. A smile, a joshing comment from Captain Murray and the newcomers were passed without challenge.

The next twenty minutes had been devoted to impromptu orientation, with Sean Toolan, Coletta Devane, Mike Kelsay and the rest of the Grey Dog squad being shown about the sprawling station to pinpoint key strike zones.

In the two computer sections regulating the flow of crude into the pipeline proper, the skimpy night crew barely gave them a passing glance.

Outside, spread over ten thousand acres, such oil giants as Sohio, BP Alaska, Exxon, Arco and Atlantic Richfield had set up miniature refineries, plush office buildings to oversee the splitting of the molasses-thick crude before it could flow into the TAP. The logistics of the baby pipeline alone were awesome.

But this was of no concern to the saboteurs. They would go for the jugular, attack the heart of the Trans-Alaska. Pumping station one. Reduce it to shambles.

As they drifted through the control rooms, the main group of the Prudhoe personnel slept elsewhere, content to entrust security to their "night people." Pumping station one breathed in torpid half-life, the mazelike corridors deserted. The generators, the compressor engines, the huge aircraft-type turbine pumps hammered drowsily, their thunder somehow muted.

In the condensing rooms, the thirty-odd stacks towering fifty feet high, a skeleton crew patrolled the catwalks, climbed steel ladders to check gauges in sleepwalker movements. Outside, clouds of steam released from the thermal-pressure section turned to instant fog, mantling the building in a comforting vapor blanket, adding to the illusion of warm, snug safety within.

Grey Dog's dirty work could have been completed in three minutes flat. But delay was integral to Grey Dog's strategy, synchronization its keynote. Everything must blow at once if they were to subvert interior security and operate right under the U.S. Army's nose up to the final countdown. Everything must happen with split-second timing.

If they were to escape Prudhoe untouched, skim

down the line to retrieve comrades at three other demolition sites, then detour to QSS 0022 to pick up the seven men there, they must generate wholesale confusion in one fell swoop. Thus, the time bomb ticked merrily, fuse set for 0200 hours.

They could afford to deploy slowly, carefully, with each man in key position. Lynch was responsible for the Yank soldiers at the entrance ways; they could not be allowed to sound alarm. Flaherty and his demolition squad would take out the master-control areas, the pumps and heat converters. Devane's party would patrol the grounds outside. On and on the assignments went.

Minute by minute, the clock hands moved forward.

And now, at 0148 hours, at each of the three main doorways, in identical sequence.... "Hey mate," the fly-boys called to the GI guards. "Could you step in here for a minute?"

Reflexes deadened by the late hour, the soldiers innocently complied. Then eyes went wide as they saw the primitive Welrod pistol, its silencer resembling a black mailing tube. And before any of them could make a retaliatory move, the antique gun coughed twice, and the soldiers were spun back, a chunk of each man's face suddenly missing.

COLONEL KATZENELENBOGEN and his four comrades were dying by inches. Never had the Bell 206L moved more slowly; never had the minutes dragged as they were just then. It was 0140, and

they were still a good sixty miles south of Prudhoe. "Grimaldi," Yakov groused, "can't we go
any faster? Certainly the Irish bastards have
started their countdown by now."

"Negative, chief," Grimaldi snapped. "A hundred forty's all she's got. I'm risking malfunction
to hold her there. Rotors'll be going on without us
if I push her any harder."

"Any chance we can head 'em off?" Manning
asked, his cold eyes feverish for a change.

"I doubt it. They're most likely blowing things
sky-high right now." His grimace was cruel. "But
we might just catch them at work. We can take it
out of their hides, at least."

Grimaldi then caught sight of what they were
looking for. "Coming up, dead ahead."

There was gradual brightening on the horizon, a
flat orange glow. Then, minutes later, pinpricks of
red, as the tips of hundred-foot-high "blow
pipes" edged across the earth's curvature. Natural
gas was being fired off at well rigs as far as the eye
could see. And dead ahead, a flat blur of white
light, the pumping station itself, floodlit twenty-
four hours a day. An oasis of light in the heart of a
universe of darkness.

"Christ, what a waste," Rafael said referring to
the burn off. "We got poor folks freezing to death
back home."

Yakov then moved into a swift recap of their attack plan. Time running out, there was no room
for cautious approach; they must launch themselves into the teeth of the enemy and hope that

the element of surprise would give them the crucial winner's edge.

"We hit the condenser section," Yakov snapped. "Land on the roof of the main building, execute a probe for a hatch of some sort. If there's nothing there, then we go over the side with the same rope that got us down. Got that?"

Everyone nodded, expressions grave.

"Rafael and Gary, you've got the control center. Keio and David, back me up in the pumping rooms. Jack, can you hold position and disconnect the cable at the same time?"

"No problem, Yakov," the pilot grinned. "What about the Army boys? They're supposed to be running patrols down there. What if they take you guys for more of the terrorist gang?"

"We'll cross that bridge when we come to it." Again he brushed in his reasons for the air drop. They might be sitting ducks, but there was still a three-hundred-foot margin of safety they would not have in a similar ground approach. And with the terrorists shooting straight up—it was a highly defensible risk.

As the chopper took a wide, curving swipe at the huge, square building, swooping down like a hungry falcon, Yakov instructed Rafael, "Make that rope fast."

Grimaldi then steadied the Long Ranger, descending in gradual steps. Encizo took a balanced stance, splayed the two-hundred-foot coil of mountaineer's rope in precise array, snapping the anchor clevis into the chute pull ring over the hatch. "Everybody cover," Katz went on. "But no shooting unless Gary draws fire from below." He signaled to Keio to begin sliding the door aside.

A blast of frigid air lashed them. Weapons were adjusted, last-minute tuggings and buttonings of winter gear seen to.

With a decisive, fluid move, Manning clamped the choke collar onto the line and jammed gloved fingers into the spring-tensioned handle. A last shrug-over with the CAR-15 strap. Then, he stepped off the edge of the bulkhead and grunted as his right arm took sudden strain. Swiftly he dropped from sight, plummeting at a dead-drop of twenty feet per second, using the line braced under his butt as a braking device—grabbing and releasing in jarring stops and starts. It was a maneuver they had spent long hours practicing at Stony Man. Then, as he neared the roof. . . .

"Hold steady, Jack," Yakov shot. "Drifting to the west. Back off ten feet."

They saw Manning drop off, roll and bob back to his feet. Sheets of vapor drifted past just then, obscuring their view. Then Manning was in sight, sending an all-clear, throwing his shoulder into the rope to steady the next man down.

"Rafael," Yakov said, not even looking, his eyes scanning the roof, the ground, for sign of Grey Dog counteraction. Rafael reflexively crossed himself, dropped, the rope singing in the wind.

Katz was next, wrapping his left hand in the D

rings, balancing with the hooks of his right as he whizzed down, moving faster than any of the others. Still there was no ground fire. Obviously the terrorists were busy with more important things at the moment. Even the earsplitting racket of an alien helicopter could not deter their bloody purpose.

"'Off we go, into the wild blue yonder...'" McCarter sang tunelessly as he went over the side.

Keio was last man down.

Above them they saw a glimmer of movement, Grimaldi at the clevis. Seconds later, the rope was floating down. The chopper lifted up as if it was attached to a pulley, and stood by to the west, holding at an even three thousand.

"Over here," Manning said, stopping Encizo's rope-coiling chores flat. "We've got a transom here. Now if we can just get it open...."

It was at that moment that Coletta Devane, trailed by two green-suited guncocks, emerged from a side door, fanning out in the yard below. Staring up at the departing hover bird, unaware that she had just missed a crucial interplay, she considered firing upon it, then changed her mind, not wanting to draw attention.

McCarter, standing watch while the rest struggled to pry the roof hatch open, saw the trio and felt his heart kick. "Hey, Yakov," he called softly. "Get this. GIs. Maybe we're not too late after all."

As Katz sidled over and took a furtive peek, one of the hardmen called to his partner, the brogue a dead giveaway. McCarter stiffened then moved to poke his AK-47 over the edge of the roof, blast them to hell. A touch on the sleeve, and his fury was reined in; he was reconciled to playing team ball.

"Of all the dumb stunts," he cursed himself. "Right ready to give 'em the old 'hi, mate' I was."

Soft mutter carried from their right, and they hurried back to find that Keio and Manning had forced the door. Stealthily Manning cracked it several inches, placed a wary eye to the narrow opening.

"Nothing but machinery down there," he reported. "I don't see a soul. Let's go."

Phoenix Force frantically clambered down the iron ladder leading from the emergency exit, the sound of their booted feet masked by the heavy throbbing of the half acre of engines within. Assault rifles at kill position, they spread out on the first catwalk, straining for sight of Irish liberation troops below. But there was only a forest of condenser stacks, a mishmash of piping and controls, the cooling stills, a line of pressure tanks that stretched two hundred feet into the distance. Heat swarmed in stultifying clouds; clothing was quickly loosened, cartridge belts and body leather adjusted. Encizo freed his knife.

But as they vigilantly worked their way to lower-level catwalks, they found they were not alone after all.

Ahead, blood dripping through the grating in steady flow, the body of a pumping-station worker was sprawled on the ramp. Three slugs had punched away the better part of his groin. And beneath him, still huddled over his desk, another man, his head welded to his paperwork with gore and brain gell. Then at the far right, near one of the three doorways, two more bodies, lying in tangled crisscross, their eyes grotesquely puddled with blood.

Cold dread descended. Time to quit fooling themselves. They *had* arrived too late.

"Dirty, murdering sewer slime," McCarter exploded.

"Freeze," Yakov warned, ducking back behind a perforated steam screen. "Somebody's coming."

From separate hiding places along the catwalk they stole glances at the two men entering at the far end of the plant, small boxes in hand. Totally confident, the terrorists looked neither up, down, right, left. They had mind only for the big bang they were in the process of building. Crouched before a central control bank, they talked softly, taping small packs of plastic explosive at vital spots.

Manning trained his CAR-15 on them and held the pose. Katz waved Encizo and Ohara forward. "Go over the top," he whispered. "No noise if at all possible. If we have any advantage it's that they don't know we're here."

"It will be easy," Keio grinned. Instantly they were stripping off their belts, depositing the rifles upon them. Knives were taken from respective sheaths.

Then they were flitting swiftly down the catwalk.

The others saw them climb atop the catwalk rail and balance momentarily. Then they dropped down, lethal sandbags.

The terrorists never knew what hit them. The air commandos brought their knees into the demo team's backs, breaking ribs as they flattened them. There was a muffled set of *whoofs*, the beginning of a terrorized outcry.

But these died aborning. The Gerber and the long blade rose then flashed down in an air-sizzling blur. Once. Twice. Into the back, into the right side, just beneath the armpit.

Keio and Rafael were still standing over their convulsing victims when the rest hurried down to join them. Encizo leaned and wiped his Gerber on the hardman's uniform. Keio followed suit.

Rafael absently strapped on the belt, shouldering the Stoner that McCarter handed him.

Manning was busily inspecting the half-finished explosive hookup. "No exterior detonators," he said thoughtfully. "Which means chemical detonation. Disengage the shield, and you've got time before the chemicals burn through to the plastique, setting off the whole thing."

"So?" Katz said.

"Timetable. That's how cocky they are. They must be planning to pull the shields at the last moment then clear out. Everything goes up five minutes after they're airborne."

"Cheeky bastards, aren't they?" McCarter interjected.

Just then Manning's theory was summarily shot to hell. Down the corridor they heard the rattle of automatic-rifle fire, flat, tearing explosions signifying grenade action. For perhaps one minute the muffled clamor carried. Then there was a haunting stillness.

But by then Phoenix was on the move. "Guess we don't have to worry about making noise anymore," Rafael growled as they eased into the dimly lit corridor that led to the master-control centers and started furtive recon.

They came to a crossroads, where another corridor bisected. "Pump rooms to the right," Yakov shouted. "Keio and McCarter. *Go*."

As they complied with his command, flinging themselves down another long, rubber-matted tunnel, Katz himself was momentarily sidetracked. Three INLAs broke from a doorway at the end of the hall and came straight at them. But before the terrorists could wipe astonishment from their faces, raise their M-16s the necessary fourteen inches to fire—

Instant massacre.

The Stoner M-63 A-1, the Uzi, the CAR-15 all bayed a sudden requiem for the terrorists, a joint spray of thirty-odd rounds stopping them in their tracks. A halo of blood seemingly exploded around them, hung in a heavy mist, splattering the walls, ceiling and floor of their impromptu funeral home with crimson spotting and streaks.

Their M-16s clattered forward, forming an additional obstacle course as Manning and Rafael threaded their way toward the nerve center, their feet sliding in warm blood.

Yakov, torn between following them and joining Keio and McCarter, finally stuck to the plan and headed for the pump area.

The firefight had barely consumed thirty seconds, and inside the computer area, the three remaining Grey Dogs were just setting up shop when the two invaders banged through the opening, sliding low, their scatterboxes thundering.

The scene confronting them was chaotic. Silicon Valley would make a mint replacing the bullet and shrapnel ravaged computers. As for the six luckless technicians who had been gunned down at their consoles—their circuit boards were down for eternity.

But this was peripheral input, for Rafael and Manning's main attention was devoted to the green-suited figures blurring on the left and right, to the rip-saw fireblasts flashing off in their eyes, to swift sideways freefall as they saw hot lead redballing their way.

As Encizo fell behind a bullet-riddled desk, flinging his arm, the green frag grenade was looping high across the room. "Down," he warned Manning, clamping hands to his ears.

The air was suddenly compressed, the metallic, shattering *kerwhump* hitting like a punch to the gut. Even with his ears protected, Rafael's head still rang. Thinking to capitalize on the concussive impact, catch the stunned survivors with their brains clanging, he peered warily up, the Stoner panning the far end of the room.

He sent off another burst of head-slicers, catching an Irish hardman in the act of throwing a frag in his direction. The 5.56mm slugs slammed his chest, spun him back. The grenade handle chattered, but the apple fell sideways, barely launched.

"Live one," Rafael yelled as he dropped, again clamping his ears.

The whump was muffled this time, but shrapnel, pieces of electronics, human flesh cascaded across the room. With a grimace Encizo whisked blood, specks of human meat off his white winter suit.

Encizo and Manning counted a slow ten before emerging from their foxholes. They heard the sparking of a short-circuited computer in the distance, the soft sounds of a human body in final death throes. Edging up very slowly, they surveyed the room.

"If computers could bleed," Manning said, his eyes sad as he regarded the microchip graveyard. "We'd be up to our ankles in it."

Slowly, rifles poised, they flanked the battle area, worked closer to view their ugly handiwork. Encizo made a sour face as he saw how the grenade had chewed up the warrior's head. It had been turned into crimson pulp, the man's features totally indistinguishable.

A second man was bent backward over a toppled chair, his chest an open pit, his face torn by shrapnel, his smile sliced from ear to ear.

Farther down the line they found a man curled into the kneehole of a desk, death peppered across his frame.

Warily Rafael and Manning edged into the hallway, alert for the slightest betraying sound. They skulked toward the second master-operations control center. Positive as they were that the recent commotion had spooked any malingerers there, they were duty bound to check just the same.

They had almost covered the fifty feet between the two nerve centers, were poised for thrust, when they heard a muffled voice carry from inside. They froze, put their backs to the wall, trigger fingers itchy.

"Throw 'em one of our avocados?" Rafael whispered.

Manning nodded.

The Cuban duck-walked as close as he dared to the door, uncapped a fresh M-26. "Heads up," he roared, and arced it into the room. The explosion jarred them even in the hall, pieces of shooting steel taking out what remained of the glass in the door.

They fell back and waited until all the shrapnel had settled. Agonized screams sounded loudly. "Let's go finish 'em off," Encizo urged.

"No, wait," Manning said, his eyes suspicious. "Something isn't ringing right here." Hastily he disengaged his parka, draped it on the barrel of his rifle. Carrying the CAR-15 at the vertical, he sidled to the edge of the casement, where the one door was jammed open.

"Duck in low," he hissed, "when I move it. Go in wide open." Rafael was poised in a semicrouch, the Stoner reloaded, on full automatic.

Manning lowered the carbine, teasingly showed the tail of the parka at the top of the opening. Immediately a hail of 5.56mm tumblers tore the fur to confetti. At which point Encizo darted forward, crashed to his belly, the Stoner bellowing. Hot lead, incoming.

He felt the death fire, definite swaths of air shunted aside by the slugs spinning just above his head. Yet he never flinched, superb reflexes all under control. The would-be ambush artists, half concealed by the same heavy oak desks that had saved them from the grenade, became faces in a shooting gallery, the Stoner chopping their heads to dog meat in the wink of an eye.

This time their screams were real.

"Close," the Cuban whistled as he guardedly entered the room, rifle panning for any other unpleasant surprises. "How come you tumbled?"

"They were yelling too loud," Manning said laconically. "Wounded men don't have that much breath left."

"Stupid asses. Must have heard our ugly music down the hall. Figured if they hid maybe it would all go away." Encizo turned one of the terrorists over with his foot.

"Kids," he grunted, making a wry face. "Neither of 'em a day over twenty." He sighed heavily. "For mother and country. What a bag of smoke that is."

They did a quick, thorough recon on the rest of the room, assessing damage. The destruction was a carbon copy of room one. Grenades for openers, rifle fire for finale. The four technicians had bought a little of both. Two were slumped over their terminals, faces in a puddle of blood, the others were shapeless rag bundles on the floor. The computer banks were a total loss.

Again the two commandos were appalled, turned thoughtful by the tragic waste the chaotic scene represented. Death, no matter how many times a man stumbles upon it, is never something one becomes hardened to. It never gets any prettier.

As quickly they shrugged off the introspections. A standing target is a dead target. A few bitter scores had already been settled. But there were more—lots more. Seconds later they broke from the temporary morgue, racing headlong down the corridor, in the direction of fresh firefight.

OUTSIDE, IN THE BONE-PULVERIZING COLD, Devane and her two accomplices continued prowling the immediate perimeter. The rumble of gunfire, the muffled thump of grenades carried from inside. But, assuming it was Toolan and company at play, they did not give it second thought. They grinned smugly to themselves, counted the minutes.

Even farther out, patrolling the outer reaches of pumping station one, an M113 APC lumbered past at fifteen miles per hour. They waved at the INLA hardmen, mistook them for their own guard detail and swept on.

At that distance the GIs certainly could not hear the bloody war raging inside the building. There was little reason to suspect anything had gone haywire. Their buddies, huddled in the station's doorways, would certainly clue them. The CP—where the rest of the Army detachment now peacefully snored away the long winter's night—would be on the horn.

Thus they rumbled on, totally oblivious. There was a sixteen-mile perimeter to patrol. They would not be by again for almost an hour. By that time the Irish terrorists would be long gone.

13

Sean Toolan raged as he cowered closer to one of the oil-flow lines, the steel warm, where preheated crude was being pressured into the main pipe. Where in hell had those bastards come from? One minute things had been going smooth, the next—unraveled. Things had come badly unraveled.

Terror crowded the Grey Dog headman's throat, touched chilled steel to his heart. It was not going to be a walk-in after all. Looking off to his right, where Derwin McSherry lay in crumpled disarray, his chest scrambled by two M-16 tumblers, his life's blood pumping out of him, Toolan was further demoralized.

He and four others had just entered the pumping rooms, had wiped out the three workmen on the graveyard shift and were dividing the plastic explosives among themselves when the two warriors in white had barged through a door at the farthest end, assault rifles blazing. Instantly, grabbing up the plastique and their weapons, they had ducked back into the maze of pipes, elbows, tanks and pressure turbines, thinking to pick off the bloody fools at leisure.

So much for complacency. It was a fool's toy. Because the intruders were pesky gnats that gave them no minute's rest. They had exchanged fire all right. And here was poor Derwin to show for it. The devil's own fighters, they were.

His panic grew, stealing his breath. His anger mounted. After all their work, after all their fine plans. . . .

"THIS BABY WON'T GO," McCarter hooted, grinning across at Ohara where he was crouched behind a heavy steel pump housing, "we'll see to that, won't we?"

Keio smiled back, sense of camaraderie very strong at that moment. "Looks like the cavalry arrived just in time."

"How many? Did you get a count?"

"Four or five at the most. I thought I saw someone in an officer's uniform. A hostage, do you think?"

"Wouldn't put it past the yellow bellies. Got a fix on any of them? Since that first lucky shot, I mean."

"Lucky shot, hell," Keio sparred. "No, they're laying low. Very low. Looks like they're bunching up on the left though."

It was then that a fleeting blur crossed an entrance way behind them. "Yakov," McCarter alerted. *"Cover."*

Both sent a fire screen toward the rear of the complex, counting on ricochets to make the terror goons kiss dirt. As Katz charged forward and deftly mounted the concrete platform upon which Mc-Carter was deployed, he was given swift fill-in. "Grenades?" he asked.

"Questionable," McCarter replied. "They've got one of the Army officers captive. Unless you figure he's expendable."

Katz pursed his lips, lapsed into thought. While he did not want to expose his team to unnecessary risk, he still wanted to protect the officer if possible. Just the same, expediency was of the essence. There was no telling when Grey Dog reinforcements might converge on this key target.

"Any chance of getting high?" Yakov suggested as Keio made a swift dash, settled in beside them. "That catwalk there."

"We'd be sitting ducks," McCarter objected.

"Not if one of us captures that observation area there." He pointed to a steel-plated control shed above. "We open up the minute our man moves. You volunteering, Keio?" he said, fixing the Oriental with a stern smile.

"Affirmative, Yakov," the martial-arts expert whipped back.

"Damned risky," McCarter scowled. "Let me go."

But Ohara was already up, loping for the steel stairs, his long body launched with catlike swiftness. "Flush them out if you can." The additional order caught him as he braced for the final rush. "We'll do our part from this end."

Then the Japanese thunderbolt was streaking up the stairs, taking three risers at a time. Yakov

flung himself to the left, deliberately coaxing fire.
The heavy rumble of the dozen pumps served to
camouflage the sound of his initial rush.

The pucky Mossad vet executed tricky grace
steps at each aisle, slamming rounds down the
line. For his part, McCarter squirmed around his
fortress, pouring more distracting slugs into the
stronghold.

Even so, the Irish were quickly alerted to a sudden eye-in-the-sky, and directed frantic bursts at
the elusive Japanese giant. Keio virtually toe-
danced through the fusillade, running flat-out, his
M-16 held high. Torn between taking him down
and protecting their own skins, the hardmen had
no time for a second try. By then Keio was safely
inside the steel cage, the half-door slammed
behind him. He collapsed to the floor, used the
time to reload.

Miraculously no one was hit in the manic ex-
change. The terrorists slammed fresh magazines
home and awaited further developments. Totally
unglued, unnerved by the bravado of their attackers, they doubted that they were equal to the
challenge thrown down.

A line of twenty huge steel elbows, partial feed-
er lines from the separate oil producers, stretched
along the far end of the pumping room. Each
eight-foot-high elbow provided excellent cover for
the hardmen. Sean Toolan had finally opted to
clear out, leave his comrades to fend for themselves. There was a door there. If he could just
break out of this stupid trap, reach Coletta. With

her men they could make a fresh stand—with infinitely better odds.

At that moment Keio popped from his airborne tollbooth, peppered four rounds of 5.56mm slugs in Toolan's direction, drove him back, definite second thoughts suddenly born. In his rage Toolan touched off a burst of his own. But by that time Keio had dropped from sight.

As the firefight continued, a voice howled from the easternmost corner of the room, the words echoing clearly. "Don't let them kill me. I'm an American officer. They're holding me prisoner. Help me, someone, please."

"You dirty, traitorous swine," an Irish voice thundered. "I'll...." The threat immediately died as David McCarter, coming from behind a series of pressure valves, surprised the INLA hardguy, putting three rounds into his back. Then he had the officer in hand and was viciously dragging him out of danger.

"Oh, Jesus Christ." Captain Murray, eternally quick on his feet, pantomimed vast relief. "I can never repay you." Yakov moved up to join them. "That was a close one, guys," he continued in flatland midwestern accent, immediately convincing them that he was authentic Government Issue. "I sure thought I was a goner. God, I can't thank you enough."

"Just hang back," Yakov cut him short, more important business at hand. "Keep out of the line of fire if you can. Leave the rest to us."

It was as both Katz and McCarter wheeled,

started back to the wars, that a sly, crazed light erupted in Captain Dan Murray's eyes. Taking a desperate, last-ditch chance....

Swiftly the Colt .45 snicked out from its side holster, the safety already off. Murray assumed the Army's two-hand stance, took careful aim—a quick one-two intended—and steadied himself for the cheap-shots of the century.

But he waited a moment too long. Suddenly, from above, came the angry stutter of an M-16. At least four rounds caught Murray in the chest and throat, while the last four all but removed the top of his skull. Brain vomit and blood exploded in a three-foot spray on both sides of the double-dealer.

"What the hell..." Yakov gasped, whirling just in time to see Murray go down, sliding two feet on the gangway before he came to a rest. As he saw the automatic still hanging from Murray's fingers, he understood Keio's swift, instinctive action. Suddenly his legs felt very wobbly.

Cautiously Keio's grinning face emerged from behind the steel screen. He sent his chief a fleeting high sign.

Katz's tight, crumpled smile, the terse nod of his head were worth all the effusive "thank-yous" in the world to the proud Japanese warrior.

The self-congratulatory mood was quickly shattered. Sean Toolan, the last living terrorist in the room, made his final, bold move. Rising from his lair among the flow-line pipes, he sent a burst of flesh-seekers at Keio Ohara, an errant wisp of an escape plan forming in his mind.

Anything was worth the risk now to the Grey Dog topcock—anything that would put distance between him and these relentless gunmen. Totally demoralized, fully aware that he was alone, at their mercy, he would grasp at any straw. They would tear him limb from limb if they got their hands on him.

But first, he adjured himself, get that miserable bastard up in the control shack. He had to die; otherwise his plan was doomed to failure. Again he hammered an eight-round line up at him. His heart soared as he saw the target drop back into his hole. There, he rejoiced, that had got him.

How close Keio came to death at that moment was very evident. That brief eye-lock with his leader had almost cost him his life.

Crouching behind the heavy steel, the lead hammering in deafening flow, stray ricochet rounds screaming past his ears, he realized that he had to act. To sit and wait for a stray slug to find him was ridiculous. In a crazed outflow of rage, he tensed, readied his M-16, prepared to answer the maddening fire.

He had barely raised an inch when McCarter roared, "Down, Keio. You want your head blown off?"

Simultaneously McCarter and Katz worked their way around their pipeline fortifications; they opened fire on the place where Toolan had just been.

Just as the INLA leader had hoped. Using the distraction to good advantage, he dropped to his belly, crawled back *toward* the enemy, swiftly losing himself in a greasy tangle of pipes and valves that effectively concealed his change in route. He had noticed another catwalk, perched even higher up than that held by the gunner. He knew he had to get there.

There was a door there that connected to the pumping station's adjoining rooms. He would be through it and gone before the attackers could collect their wits. If only he could be positive one of his rounds had put down that gunner for good.

Sean Toolan had, in his youth, served a stint in a steel manufacturing plant in Dublin; he knew how an electric winch worked. He knew how startlingly swift the hook could be made to rise—if there were no real loads involved.

And here, within easy striking distance, on the far side of the central catwalk—a winch of winches, overpowered, with the most modern, most responsive of controls. These damned Americans did things right sometimes.

Grunting, terror continuing to lash him, he jammed his lean body beneath an especially low-hanging set of piping and vent work, the tracked winch that much closer now. Masked by the roar of the machinery, the clamor of the Yank attack force's weapons, the winch's electric hum would hardly register.

Yakov and McCarter, infiltrating deeper into the west end of the room, firing sporadically to keep their quarry in place, played right into Sean

Toolan's hands. "Come on out, you bucket of
Irish shit," McCarter taunted.

Fresh hatred curdled Toolan's guts. An English
toff was it? A bloody Brit. Could anything be
sweeter than the death of a Brit?

The platform where the flexible control cable
hung was one guarded lunge away.

He heard the men grumbling between themselves, the random spatter of rounds—one covering the other—as they moved closer. Then,
decisively, breaking out from beneath a roof of
multiple runs of pipe, his M-16 panning to the left,
Toolan padded across the steel deck. He swiftly
placed his left foot into the curve of the hook, set
his right on the sharp point for balance.

Still, as he drew in the control box, switched the
power on, last-minute doubts struck. He would be
a sure bull's-eye. Up in the air on a string like that.
It was a chance he would have to take. His only
chance. At least he would die like a man, fighting,
risking everything. He would not wait in some
bloody hole for them to come and blow his head
away. No.

Besides, there was the element of surprise to
consider. Their backs to him, thinking they had
him cornered, which of them would think to
watch overhead? And once he gained that upper
catwalk, he would cut them to ribbons.

He touched the Up button, wrapped his left arm
around the grease-slicked cable. Instantly he
began a slow ascent, his eyes darting between the
two men on the floor and the iron coffin occupied

by the gunner—who he was now positive was dead. There had been no sign of any movement for several minutes on that front. The bastard had to be dead.

But Keio was not dead. Badly shocked perhaps, dazed to near insensibility by the head-splitting clangor of M-16 tumblers on boiler plate. The chilling significance of the near misses had not helped either. His brain clouded, he vaguely heard the shooting below and convinced himself that Yakov and McCarter had things under control. It would be a mere matter of minutes before they moved in for the kill.

They ordered him to stay down. And until he heard that final all clear, he would follow orders, like the good soldier he was.

But then, cutting through his fog, came the dull whine of the motorized overhead pulley. What the hell, he wondered, shaking his head to clear it. He half raised himself, groggily eased his eyes over the rim of the gate for fleeting seconds, dropped back again, his heart suddenly pounding.

Not more than fifteen feet above him, rising fast, his M-16 trained on the area where Yakov and McCarter were moving up, was the Grey Dog headman.

Toolan, already discounting the gunner he thought he had killed, intent on the two whitesuits flanking the array of elbows, never saw Keio as he floated up in his cage. His face in an agonized grimace, Keio knew his opening blast had to be true. Should he miss, one checkout burst by Toolan would take out Katz or McCarter—or both—for good.

He shot Toolan in the hands, the slugs hammering Toolan's rifle from his grip, hoping to spin him off the cable at the same time. The M-16 chewed out lead in six quick spurts, the reports rebounding off the walls with startling force. On the floor, Yakov and McCarter spun and stared up with disbelieving eyes. As they brought up their weapons, Keio pumped another half-dozen tumblers into Toolan. The hook froze in space.

But the terrorist was tough. Even as life's last oath was jarred from his throat, the M-16 instantly dropped, the man's arms reflexively closed on the steel cable. What was left of his left hand clamped down with steely power. Even when his feet slipped from the hook, flopped in empty air, he still hung on.

McCarter and Katz raised their weapons, added their own thunder to the execution.

At long last the hardman's arms and fingers relaxed. The body slid down the cable.

But even here Sean Toolan was denied the dignity he had so diligently sought all his life. For, in final freefall his head connected with the hook. The speed of his descent literally rammed the jut of his chin against the shaft, flopping his head back. The point of the hook slashed into the V of his jawbone, tore through the flesh, penetrated his mouth, stopped his plunge with neck-snapping abruptness.

There, swaying slowly like a spiked side of beef

in a storage locker, he was suspended forty feet above their heads.

Only then, the last rounds going nowhere, did McCarter finally stop shooting. His face twisted in sick revulsion, he could not take his eyes from the swinging body.

But even so there was no time for breathing space.

For just then there was a commotion in the hallway to their left. They whirled, dropped back into their pipe stockade, brought rifles instantly to bear.

All released ponderous sighs of relief as Encizo's face cautiously poked itself around the edge of the door frame.

Then, as he and Manning entered the slaughterhouse, saw the queasiness on the faces of their comrades, they both glanced up, took in the grisly gallows.

Encizo's jaw gaped, his eyes went wide. "Mother of God!" he blurted. "How'n hell did you guys manage to do that?"

14

Again Phoenix Force was on the prowl.

Spread out, branching into the myriad corridors and stairwells the pumping station boasted, they moved like phantoms as they sought to flush the last Grey Dog remnants. Once more they sadly surveyed the mayhem in the master-control centers, stepping over the bodies of the trio sprawled in the hall on their way in, again on their way out. Next they rechecked the compressor area.

Upstairs they searched deserted, dark office units, each new door-opening a separate maneuver. Lights flashed on, assault rifles panned with desperate swiftness, breaths were drawn back sharply. But always, no sign of any cowering terrorists.

There was a fresh lightness to their stride as they came down the stairs, all assured that their ugly work was near an end.

"Our friend on the hook," Manning remarked as they came down the stairs for the second time, "he must have been the last of the scuzzy lot."

"Hardly," Katz answered. "Those people outside, remember? Unless they came in to get warm. They can wait. Until we're absolutely sure everyone's cleaned out in here. We'll go out after them together."

He paused in mid-stride. "In the meantime, the generator complex. We haven't checked that yet. Can you men handle it without me? I should be seeing to raising somebody over in the billeting buildings, at the Army CP. If any of these phones are still operative." He winked. "Seems to me we could use a little help about now."

"That'll be the day," McCarter hooted.

"Keep your guard up," Katz warned as he turned, started off to find a telephone.

"Right-o," McCarter snapped. "C'mon, mates."

But, as they progressed down the corridor, advancing more carelessly than was wise, boots clumping, rifles slung over their shoulders, they could not resist the temptation to peek into the pumping rooms one last time. They wanted one last look at the bastard who had almost cost them their lives.

One by one they filed into the room, stood in a loose semicircle, stared up at Toolan's suspended body for long moments. Lost in grim reverie, nobody venturing a comment, they were perfect patsies for what happened.

"Stand right there," the strident female voice barked from behind them, the suddenness of it jarring them with all the impact of a kick in the groin. "Don't move, or we'll blow your goddamned heads off."

All four men froze, feeling a paralyzing chill

claw through their guts. To a man they cursed themselves for fools, for allowing themselves to become overconfident.

"Dick, you and Clancy get their weapons," the harsh voice commanded. "Then we'll take the devil's sweet time settling scores for what they did to poor Sean."

The two Grey Dogs, mature, war-savvy specimens, prodded them in the back with the muzzles of their M-16s. "Drop the guns, you bastards," one of them growled. "No tricks...."

One by one the rifles dropped to the floor. But the terrorists did not move to frisk Phoenix for small arms. There was, perhaps, a light after all. But even as hope flared, it died. Fat chance, with all those clothes in the way.

"Turn around now, damn you. I want you all to see it comin' when you get it."

And there, standing half concealed behind a steel heat shield—

The woman's parka was flung back, revealing the full glory of her long, red hair. Despite the demented, vengeful glitter in her eyes, she was a beautiful creature. Recalling the man they so recently had seen tied to the bunk at the satellite tracking base, their desolation deepened. If ever the men of Phoenix were to know the hell of terror, then this, most certainly, was it.

"Had yourselves a bit of sport with my Sean, did you?" the copper-tressed woman grated, drawing her lips back over her teeth. "Animals. Animals is what you are."

None of them made any move to answer, to attempt an explanation of the terrorist leader's grotesque death. They would not grant the woman even that satisfaction. They stared stolidly, eyes darting, seeking an opening. Odds of any sort. A thousand-to-one. Anything.

Now her face went sly, as if sensing that time was getting away on her. If they were to somehow effect an escape.... Finish them off, but fast.

"Dick. You, Clancy. When I count three. In the ballocks, do you hear? A fine stand of geldings we'll have. It's what they deserve. Even if they live, they'll be sorry the longest day they live."

Her voice became even more maniacal. "For you, Sean," she wailed. "Saints in heaven, Sean, are you watching? Forgive me, darling. Forgive me for the shame I put upon you...."

The men of Phoenix Force were as taut as bowstrings, their jaws tensed to breaking point as they waited for the rifles to spill their hot, tearing tissue. They waited in despair for any shred of distraction that would permit them to charge the bloodthirsty trio. One thing was certain—they would not just stand there and let the deranged swine cut them down.

"Here's sport for you, boys," Coletta Devane shrieked. "Ready, Dick and Clancy. When I...."

The sentence was never finished. For just then the world exploded off to the madwoman's right. Suddenly Katzenelenbogen was there, feet firmly planted, the Uzi spitting nonstop death.

Keio, McCarter, Rafael and Manning hit the

dirt, random slugs from the terrorists' M-16s whining above their heads, trigger fingers popping off rounds even as their owners jerked and writhed, went into a last, spinning dance of death.

With instinctive skill the Israeli had placed himself so that his line of fire would slice each head at once; no skull would be allowed to form a shield for the next.

Blood, charges of gray brain matter and bone were flung to the left. Devane's lovely face was turned to gaping, bloody craters.

The first to go down, she landed on her back, her arms and legs at crazy angle. Clancy Dolan was sprawled on top of her. Even in death. . . .

Even when the Uzi's high-pitched chatter finally died, the four Phoenix Force members still lay in a stunned, awkward sprawl, as if momentarily turned to stone. No smart talk now. No talk at all. Each was too preoccupied, too busy digesting a bitter lesson in humility that he would not forget as long as he lived.

And where there should have been curt recrimination from Yakov, there was none. For he, too, was stricken, and stood silent, unable to take his eyes off of what was left of Coletta Devane's face. The cascade of rust-colored hair about that pulpy mass of gore became particularly devastating.

"My God," he said in a hushed, awed voice, "this is the first time in my life I ever shot a woman. . . ."

15

"And speaking of the Irish," David McCarter laughed as he put down his glass of rum and Coke, "as I'm sure we were.... Do you know the one about John Dunn and his trip to America?"

Keio pulled a long face. "We don't need Irish jokes."

"Go ahead," Manning encouraged. "I haven't heard it."

It was midafternoon, and now—two days after their brush with death—in a Klondike-style saloon located on Fairbanks's notorious "Two Street," the Phoenix team killed time while waiting for a flight to Washington, D.C.—and Stony Man. It was 1400 hours. Their flight was scheduled for 1630. There was time for letdown; anything that would elevate their mood after the grim happenings of the past days was more than welcome.

Dressed in civilian clothes, giving illusion of harmless vulnerability, they were gathered about a round oak table, glasses and bottles spread across its battered surface. They had earned it, and they were damned well going to enjoy it. Even if they had to be poured onto the plane.

Encizo had a squat glass of brandy before him

and was chasing it with beer. Yakov was nursing a Scotch on the rocks, while Gary Manning was developing a pleasant glow on Scotch and water. Ohara, the most moderate of the lot, was working on a glass of Burgundy. McCarter had his usual Coke, to which he was adding generous amounts of rum.

"There was this bloke named Pat O'Malley," McCarter began the joke, "and he was leaving Ireland for a jaunt to the United States. And just before he left, the Widow Dunn got in touch with him."

McCarter's voice slid into rich Irish brogue in all the right places, and shortly he had them all hooked. "'Me son, John, went to New York twenty years ago,' Mrs. Dunn said, 'and I ain't had no word from him ever since. I'm wonderin' whatever become of the lad.'

"She then wanted to know if Pat O'Malley would look up her son in New York and ask him to write his poor old mother back in Ireland. Pat protested that New York was an awful big place, that his chances of finding John Dunn were practically nil. Well, would he at least try? Yes, he would.

"And there was Pat on his second day in New York. Looking up, he saw this sign that said Dun & Bradstreet. The luck of the Irish, he thought. I've found the boy straight off. Entering the plush offices, he asked the pretty receptionist if they had a John there. 'Yes,' she replied, 'down the hall, second door on the right.'

"But upon entering the room Pat was at an extreme loss, for all he saw were sinks and urinals and rows of booths. Undaunted, he looked about until he saw a man's feet in the third stall down.

"So he goes down there and knocks on the door of that stall," McCarter continued, in full flow now. "And he says, 'Are you Dunn?' And the man answers, 'Yes.'

" 'Well, dammit, lad,' " McCarter said, delivering the punch line, " 'why'n hell don't ye write to y'r mother?' "

The four men were convulsed. Encizo pounded on the table, laughed until tears came to his eyes. McCarter, pleased with himself, laughed just as hard.

The uproar at their table caused some of the twenty or so locals scattered at the bar to glance their way, their expressions unquestionably hostile. Damned tourists, their eyes said.

Phoenix Force was winding down.

For the moment Prudhoe Bay was put out of their minds. Each sensed deep satisfaction in knowing that their life-and-death efforts had saved the Trans-Alaska Pipeline. The crude would be flowing before the week was out. Indeed, oil was flowing now, but sluggishly. There had been an eleven-day grace period before the 9.2 million barrels of oil in the line turned to Silly Putty. As it had developed, they needed less than a third of that time before the line would be fully operational again.

But had the INLA splinter group been successful in rupturing the TAP itself, it would have been quite a different story. Disaster of irreconcilable proportions.

Alerted in time, the Prudhoe engineers had been able to activate backup override systems at the last possible minute. Even with the computers down at both ends of the line there were manual alternatives available. The pumps, running at diminished strength, were able to generate enough pressure to push steadily to pumping stations two and three. Here, the pressure doubled and tripled, they were able to ram it over the Atigun Saddle. Home free.

Granted, there was no leeway whatsoever for new emergencies. With the sophisticated oil-flow computers at Valdez totally destroyed, a new rupture anywhere in the line would mean more problems. The seventy-one gate valves, the eighty check valves that kept the oil from backing up in the line; that diverted oil into huge storage reservoirs at each pumping station; that allowed complete bypass of the station itself if necessary—all were dependent on the Valdez computers.

These magic boxes would be out for weeks, despite round-the-clock efforts of high-tech crews jetted in from California to jerry-rig standby equipment, to replace that beyond repair. The Grey Dog hit team—all tracked down, killed in the wake of mass panic—had truly done a job at Valdez.

The same for Prudhoe. But here the destruction had not been quite as critical. Again there was undirected thanks to the phantom force that had mysteriously intervened at the crucial last minute, and had completed its bloody task so efficiently.

Just hauling away the mass of liberation army bodies at Prudhoe, along the line, back at QSS 0022, had been a job in itself.

Even Grimaldi had, at the last, gotten into the act. Flagged in without a murmur by the air-control boys, he had barely set down than he had seized one of the Ingrams, had attacked the waiting Chinook 47-C. The cowardly Grey Dog pilot had given up without firing a shot.

It had been that same pilot who had given Harrington and the other Prudhoe nabobs cause to seek the "inside" terrorist contacts. Captain Murray had been jolt enough, but when intensive scrutiny had flushed out Chief Engineer Fred Avancini, taking him into custody just as he was about to depart for a rush Riviera holiday, the net was complete.

A new gusher was discovered on the North Slope. The entire espionage cell was uncovered, and swift arrests had followed at Valdez, Fort Greely and Eileson AFB.

But, dig as they might, they could uncover nothing further about the five-man strike force that had so mysteriously moved in their midst for seven fleeting days. They were gone. Even the elusive pilot had vanished, the deserted Bell 206L— swiftly stripped of personalized arsenal—being the only evidence that he—or they—had even really existed.

Major Sam Harrington, of course, was saying

nothing. Clark Jessup, the Pentagon liaison, was long gone.

Perhaps they had imagined the whole thing.

No. For at that same moment, in a scruffy saloon in far off Fairbanks, celebrating a slightly delayed New Year's Eve. . . .

Phoenix Force was becoming quite mellow.

PHOENIX FORCE

AN EXECUTIONER SERIES

#7 Dragon's Kill

MORE GREAT ACTION COMING SOON!

The Japanese Red Cell had discovered a method of extracting information from *any* subject. The terrorists had kidnapped two American Intelligence officers in Hawaii, drained them of their secrets, then used the information to commit barbarous acts of sabotage.

Mack Bolan's ace action team, Phoenix Force, was unleashed across the Pacific with orders to destroy the cancerous Communist commandos.

Phoenix Force must hit. Hard. Fast.

And hit they did!

Mack Bolan's

PHOENIX FORCE

AN EXECUTIONER SERIES

by Gar Wilson

Phoenix Force is The Executioner's five-man army that blazes through the dirtiest of encounters. Like commandos who fight for the love of battle and the righteous unfolding of the logic of war, Bolan's five hardasses make mincemeat out of their enemies. Catch up on the whole series now!

"Strong-willed and true. Gold Eagle Books are making history. Full of adventure, daring and action!"

—*Marketing Bestsellers*

#1 **Argentine Deadline**   #4 **Tigers of Justice**
#2 **Guerilla Games**   #5 **The Fury Bombs**
#3 **Atlantic Scramble**

Phoenix Force titles are available wherever paperbacks are sold.

GOLD EAGLE

HE'S EXPLOSIVE.
HE'S UNSTOPPABLE.
HE'S MACK BOLAN!

He learned his deadly skills in Vietnam…then put them to use by destroying the Mafia in a blazing one-man war. Now **Mack Bolan** is back to battle new threats to freedom, the enemies of justice and democracy—and he's recruited some high-powered combat teams to help. **Able Team**—Bolan's famous Death Squad, now reborn to tackle urban savagery too vicious for regular law enforcement. And **Phoenix Force**—five extraordinary warriors handpicked by Bolan to fight the dirtiest of anti-terrorist wars around the world.

Fight alongside these three courageous forces for freedom in all-new, pulse-pounding action-adventure novels! Travel to the jungles of South America, the scorching sands of the Sahara and the desolate mountains of Turkey. And feel the pressure and excitement building page after page, with nonstop action that keeps you enthralled until the explosive conclusion! Yes, Mack Bolan and his combat teams are living large…and they'll fight against all odds to protect our way of life!

Now you can have all the new Executioner novels delivered right to your home!

You won't want to miss a single one of these exciting new action-adventures. And you don't have to! Just fill out and mail the coupon following and we'll enter your name in the Executioner home subscription plan. You'll then receive four brand-new action-packed books in the Executioner series every other month, delivered right to your home! You'll get two **Mack Bolan** novels, one **Able Team** and one **Phoenix Force**. No need to worry about sellouts at the bookstore…you'll receive the latest books by mail as soon as they come off the presses. That's four enthralling action novels every other month, featuring all three of the exciting series included in The Executioner library. Mail the card today to start your adventure.

FREE! Mack Bolan bumper sticker.

When we receive your card we'll send your four explosive Executioner novels and, absolutely FREE, a Mack Bolan "Live Large" bumper sticker! This large, colorful bumper sticker will look great on your car, your bulletin board, or anywhere else you want people to know that you like to "Live Large." And you are under no obligation to buy anything—because your first four books come on a 10-day free trial! If you're not thrilled with these four exciting books, just return them to us and you'll owe nothing. The bumper sticker is yours to keep, FREE!

Don't miss a single one of these thrilling novels…mail the card now, while you're thinking about it. And get the Mack Bolan bumper sticker FREE!

BOLAN FIGHTS
AGAINST ALL ODDS
TO DEFEND FREEDOM!

Mail this coupon today!